000 INDEPENDENT
000 LEGIONS
PUBLISHING

DARK MARY
by PAOLO DI ORAZIO

ISBN: 978-88-31959-20-9
DECEMBER 2018

TRANSLATION BY PAOLO DI ORAZIO, EDITED BY DANIELE BONFANTI
COPY EDITING: MICHAEL BAILEY
COORDINATION AND SUPERVISORY: ALESSANDRO MANZETTI
FRONT COVER ART: WENDY SABER CORE
REAR COVER ART AND INTERIOR ILLUSTRATIONS: PAOLO DI ORAZIO
INTERIOR COMICS:
ILLUSTRATED BY DIANA MERCOLINI, WRITTEN BY PAOLO DI ORAZIO,

Horror Writers
ASSOCIATION
SPECIALTY PRESS AWARD RECIPIENT

SUMMARY

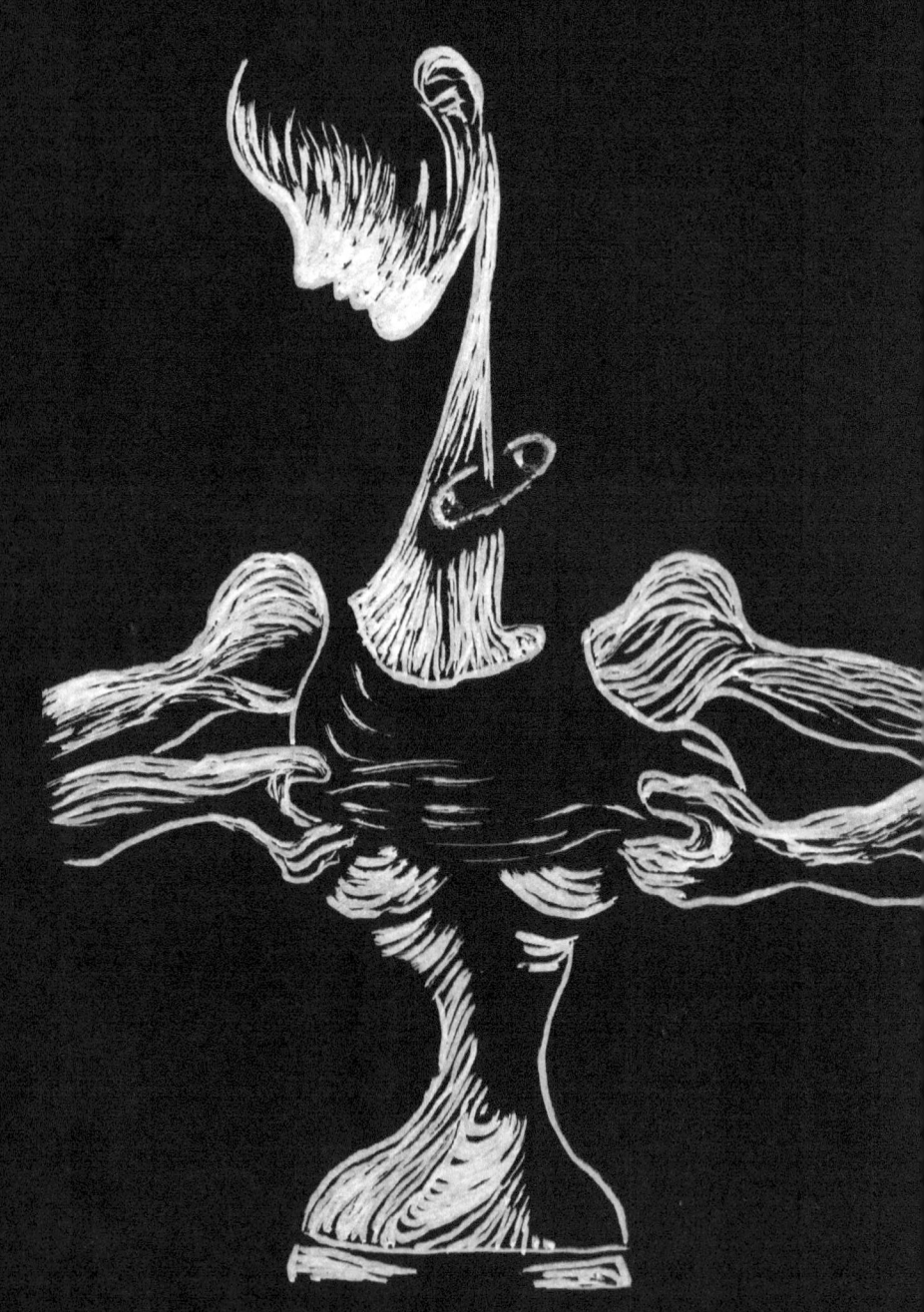

DARK MARY

PROLOGUE

Should anyone dare ask if you believe rock music really is the devil's fellow, please forget about any seventies' middle-class Catholic mindset, and take a simple look inside rock before giving any answer.

You only have to look at rock itself, at its core.

All you need to do is write down in italics – or type, using a small, rounded font – the names of the three greatest hard rock bands of all time, leaving plenty of space between letters.

Once you have done that, take a closer look at those names without reading. Look at them again. And again. And again.

Led Zeppelin

Deep Purple

Black Sabbath

Analyze these three names.

Forget what they mean.

Just keep watching the letters of these six words, and focus on their vocals and consonants. Stare as though you're supposed to be hypnotized by them.

Not immediately, but slowly, something organized will surface in your brain, a sort of *cabala* turning alphabet into numbers. It's almost like digging out an ancient message; while you're breaking up these bands' names, so different from one another, you will discover each contains the same vocal repeated thrice: *e* or *a*.

Now, erase all the other letters and look again:

ɛ   ɛ   ɛ

ɛ ɛ   ɛ

ɔ   ɔ   ɔ

Now, group together the repeating vocals.

ɛɛɛ

ɔɔɔ

Flip and reverse, until you get …

ɔ ɔ ɔ

PART ONE
HEADBANGING

The Main House Room is chock-full. A brand new deejay is playing at the Alpheus Club. Her name's Dark Mary, and she's the hottest heavy metal and hard rock stoner-girl in town.

Seven hundred people squeezed to death, dancing and jumping as if their mass movement should turn the wheels of a tank heading toward hell.

No more air in there, no more oxygen. Only sweat and noise. Noise. Noise.

Under the stage, a boy wearing torn jeans and a leather vest, totally high, leans back on the left-side subwoofer as Mary is playing "The Drug" by Warrior Soul at 110 dB. A stunning, simple coincidence. Suddenly, the boy falls to the floor, kidneys and spleen pulped by the sonic waves of bass. Unaware, Mary moves gently in a sort of smooth and slow Zen dance, in contrast with the die-cast speed of her music. She drives the playlist wearing her Pioneer headphones, a true relic of the 80s, spiral cable and volume knobs on both earpieces. She wears a small, black, see-through, total-body crocheted outfit. Doctor Martens' combat boots with heels, Jenna Style model, size 6.5. Burgundy-red Nuance lipstick on pastel-pink Max Factor, and bloody-red Zeiss contact lenses. As a tribute to Coverdale's Whitesnake, under her long black smooth hair – masked with pure indigo Sitarama henna – the sweet David creeps all around her neck, a four-foot albino python tasting the sweat-soaked air with tired curiosity, rattling its pronged tongue and capturing the massive sound vibrations in its nostrils.

From the large stage, deeply absorbed in her headphones, Dark Mary plays MP3's, cutting out the real world and pumping out songs to follow the ecstatic rumbling dance of her crowd.

Dark Mary has quickly become a real mass-attraction art-music show, a living place of worship, a no-label trend for rave parties. A noise goddess.

As a bunch of metal-heads gathers around the boy collapsed in front of the subwoofer, an out-of-order guy says *hello* to the security personnel at the stage front, then climbs the back ladder to reach Mary. She is playing Ted Nugent's "Cat Scratch Fever" from prehistoric *Double Live Gonzo*. Mary recognizes him; he's a fan. Wealthy radical-dandy straight from Parioli district – vicious, plastic-faced, blonde-haired; absolute metal layman. He does not hear the music, much less listens to it; he cares about nothing there but Dark Mary. He's here for some Dark Cunt. He has phoned and sent several emails during night broadcasts hosted by Mary – in sepulchral, no-word silence – on Radio Rock Station. But Mary actually doesn't care too much for talking. This guy, instead, seems to love stalking. This is the third night he gets too close to the deejay while she's playing her set. He doesn't give a fuck about what she's doing. He seems deaf to the sound, and blind to the strobe lights. Courteous, he looks like a fool in his short-sleeved pink shirt, blue satin tie, white linen trousers, and brown loafers at his feet with no socks, ready for *Happy Days* casting in the middle of that horde of headbangers in black. A living contradiction with his David Sylvian hairdo, *Gentlemen Take Polaroids* era.

"Hi, Mary. Great night, isn't it?" he says loudly after approaching her. He has waited for her to lift one earpiece, a green light to talk.

"Excellent. How about you?"

"I'm all right, thanks. Your set's packing a real punch," he says.

"Thanks," she says, pleased, never looking away from her two MacBook Pros – the twin cannons she uses to pilot her roaring playlist.

Dazed in the dance room, floating like a thinking buoy on the frenzied human mass, Martyna watches Mary and that freaky fan chatting. She can't stand that guy around her Mary. Of course, he has to get close to talk to her in that noise, but he's *too* fucking close. Mary's popularity is growing fast; she has many fans who love her. DMj is the latest discovery of Prince Faster – Radio Rock's deejay guru since 1983. She is the reanimator of Rome's metal army – a town where all the headbangers hide out of sight. Her metal-dance nights, her look itself, call for ever wider audiences from other cities, thanks to a devastating, cool, shocking, contagious playlist. Dark Mary's DJ-sets catch everybody: metal-heads, rockers, punkers, skaters, bikers. Even Mario and Micaela, a notorious skinhead couple next to a Hare Krishna conversion, can't lose one of her nights. Everyone wants a selfie with Maryjay for Facebook, Twitter, Instagram and Pinterest. They ask for autographs on any surface: shirts, bags, backpacks, CDs, LPs, Moleskins, helmets. The most addicted fellows ask either for a writing on skin, with toxic marker pens, or for a DMj cutter-made scarification. Mary never says no. And not only because she doesn't love to talk.

It's a really hot night. It's 1:28. Mary made her overture with "Paranoid," a deadly cover version by Megadeth. Followed by Greenday's "American Idiot," Ramones' "Rockaway Beach," Billy Idol's "Rebel Yell," stopping the chorus to let the crowd sing, "More, more, more" – just like a gig. The beat slows down with "Sleeping My Day Away" by D.A.D., "Let It Go" by Def Leppard, "Tease Me Please Me" by Scorpions, Saxon's "747 (Strangers in The Night)," Metallica's "Enter Sandman," until "Cat Scratch Fever" – time for the dandy arrival, Martyna's hated one. They are many, uncountable, and they all want to get close to Dark Mary, looking for sex. But her red contact lenses, as well as the presence of Dave-the-snake as a crawling necklace, turn every sexual plans into quick, easy conversation about music. Mary has a few words for them all – equally disapproved by Martyna, who watches and scans anyone hovering around her beloved. Driven by a flaming jealousy, she'd like to destroy them all, one by one. They only have to touch her.

As Ted Nugent keeps playing, that dandy boy is giving Mary a beer, and a 70s comic book he bought for her on eBay. He already did so three fucking times. Just as the music gets slower and the mass tension drops a bit. This shit again … to Martyna, this clearly looks like a courtship ritual. The boy pops out of nothingness and walks on stage to reach Mary and bring gifts, and talks to her. Then he says *bye* and goes away, disappearing among the mass.

Just when it's time for Rammstein's most crushing "Amerika."

The Alpheus is one of the best places in Rome to listen to live music and DJ sets. There are also conference areas, movie projections, exhibitions, two cocktail bars, and three concert halls, including the largest, the Main House Room, which hosts bands and artists of all ranks: from the famous Diaframma of Florence, to Richard Benson, no-metal guitarist who animates nihilistic performances instigating the audience to throw everything at him: coins, bottles, dead chickens.

Dark Mary plays her favorite songs, as always, pretty much for her own pleasure, which results in polarizing three thousand people per weekend. Places hosting Mary can make tens of thousands of euros a night – 2,000 going to DMj. A better deal than with any band.

Tonight, after the quick visit of the dandy guy, Dark Mary sets fire to the electrical storm and lets a remix of "Chaos A.D." by Sepultura ride on their heads. And then "Spellbound" by Siouxsie & the Banshees, "Cretin Hop" by Ramones, and "Rusty Cage" by Soundgarden. The fury decelerates to heavy doom omen with "Follow the Tears" by Heaven and Hell, and then speeds up again with Billy Idol's cyber-dance "Shock the System" and "Sweet Little Sister" by Skid Row, "Kickstart My Heart" screamed by Motley Crue, "Neon Knights" by Black Sabbath, and Megadeth's "Hangar 18." The sound pressure is pushed up to 140 decibels, pumping medium-low frequencies to highlight bass and drums beyond human endurance.

Nobody can hear the walls creaking.

Now, the dandy lover from Parioli appears and disappears, among sweaty human waves, at the peak of the sonic massacre under the strobe lights. Martyna keeps an eye on him. Steadily. This guy is not a snob at all, or maybe he is so much as to completely ignore the zoo around him, cheekily walking through the alien crowd in spite of the astonished glances from all the metal hippies and disgusted punkers.

And David doesn't seem to hinder his plans at all. Maybe, at home, he jerks off thinking about fucking the slender and nervous

Mary with the snake coldly crawling on his naked back, and feeling the beast bite his nape to death when he comes inside her.

Whatever he wants, he got close to Mary. He got close three times.

Really *too many*.

AFTER THE FIRST NIGHT OF FULL MOON: SATURDAY, 3RD OF JULY

Bodies are not pretty to look at. You have to learn how to watch them. A matter of minutes.

Rome, South West.

District XV.

Cold dawn upon the Tiber's banks. Just under the old slaughterhouse of the city, Testaccio quarter – now a fine arts center.

Senses are a fog, getting thicker, from grey to bright white until it explodes in a clot of colors. Meanwhile, a viscid squeaking – sound of working jaws – creeps inside his head. Alberto begins to wake, facedown the ground.

Half his face is deep in the mud and grass; the other half is covered by several mouths of big rats that, disgustingly quivering, feed on his tender cheeks and lips. They are ripping off his nose; the left ear, too. Pushing hard with his hands on the dirt, Alberto tries to detach from the ground, head spinning round as a carousel. The rats had taken him for a corpse, so as soon as he moves they run away. Blood is a sticky film covering his face, but Alberto cannot feel it. He breathes, and coughs up lumps of mucus and plasma. Then he stands, trying to sweep off mud and dirt. Seven hungry seagulls look at him from a distance; they would have eaten him if he were dead, pecking his back to the bone. The young man struggles to rise on his legs. Some motor deficit informs him that the deep gashes on his legs must be the reason for awakening in the company of rats. Trying to stand is a real effort because his muscles won't work with his joints any longer.

Under his ripped white trousers, the swollen lips of wounded flesh smile obliquely. The cuts, clean and deep, multiply in groups of three or four furrows. On his chest, too, and arms. Of his pink shirt, there is a memory now: a few stipes still visible among dangling pieces of skin, soaked in red and black fluid. Alberto doesn't remember getting into a knife fight, but his body is virtually cut in slices. He feels no pain as he moves. He wants to cry, but suddenly he no longer wants it. Like a broken accordion. He wants to laugh, but suddenly no longer wants to.

Alberto drags himself toward the river bank, across wiregrass and green canes on the mud. The foam of the poisoned water dances a silly waltz. Three swirls pass by like UFO sentries on the greyish Tiber's surface. Alberto searches a clean spot of shore to look at his face on the water, and to rinse it. As the cars run on the bridge above, a mosquito party is going on around Alberto and his flesh the rats have left uneaten.

There is little left of his face. The dirty water shows him in a sorry state. He looks like he's dead.

The skin of his face is sliced in ribbons and nibbled. An eye, crossed by a furrow, has exploded. His pierced and chewed cheeks reveal his teeth. Alberto's brain doesn't lose clarity.

It seems that a roller made of blades has run him over.

He doesn't remember. He doesn't remember what the hell happened.

He needs to climb the river banks in search of some help. He feels no pain – maybe because of the vast web of deep wounds all over his skin, clogged by coagulated blood; maybe for the infections that are starting to erupt from the deep.

Cold air enters the countless flesh openings, especially those in his back.

Morning sticks in its fingers to reach Alberto's soul, burning.

The sun is warming him, although the air is still cool.

Car exhaust is the good morning out of a leaden nightmare.

Alberto must reach the nearest hospital.

Industrie Bridge, along Porto Fluviale Street, is crowded with fast traffic, preventing him from walking to the opposite sidewalk. On a store window, Alberto's reflection is disgusting. He could be mistaken for a leper who just came out of a brawl. He leans against the wall, trying to elude the glances of two passersby. A woman is walking toward him. A couple seconds before getting too close, she turns, getting on the crosswalk. The cars stop. Alberto hurries behind her, but the drivers restart immediately as the woman walks across. He isn't quick enough – and now he's stuck in the middle of some crazy traffic with cars zooming around him in both directions. He must dodge like a fool, because the drivers don't seem to see him at all. Unbelievable – no mercy for Alberto. By sheer luck, his body keeps standing. Somehow, his wounds open and close at every step, letting him move almost like a normal person.

A Rottweiler furiously barks. It's mad at Alberto, and pulls its owner by the leash.

The traffic assaults Alberto again. The dog waits, looking forward to the slaughter.

A gasoline truck stops at the crosswalk to let man and dog pass. Alberto takes the opportunity to cross the street. He avoids the dog's bites. Teeth pierce the air while the animal's growls are choked by its owner's yanks.

"Hold that mutt," Alberto cries, gurgling a slimy noise through ripped lips and cheeks.

The man with the dog, busy at pulling the leash, doesn't even look at him. "Stop, Cesare. What the fuck are you doing?"

Alberto starts walking toward Portuense Road, built by Emperor Claudio, which leads out of the city and to Fiumicino Airport. He seems to remember a hospital farther that way. The unrelenting traffic runs beside him, but for the walking boy it has become like a wide-screen movie.

Emergency Room, San Camillo Hospital.

None of the waiting patients look at his face.

Maybe for the stink of blood. Or maybe he has shat his pants. That's why he feels that cold lump between his legs. It's 8:30 a.m., and a biker comes along on a stretcher with blood spilling from under his helmet. After him, two old men: the first is greenish-skinned, the second purplish. The doctors don't look at Alberto, either, though he keeps raising an arm to be noticed.

He's torn to shreds.

How is it possible no one sees me?
Too much silence, too much stillness in there. The place gets on his nerves, save for the palm trees in the courtyard.
Better to leave.

He's hungry, now.
The wounds. About thirty only on his chest. Among the tangle of gashes, red and smooth craters sparkle, circled by thin and deep grooves. A dog has bitten away his belly; that's clear. His hips and loins as well show similar, horrid marks. Every single tender part of him has been snapped and torn. He doesn't care who or what did that to him, but he can't explain how he's still alive.
Alberto is not a physician, but he can guess he has lost a lot of blood.
He feels dizzy.
A snack bar.
Must eat something.
He drags himself barefoot between rows of parked cars. Strong, warm croissant aroma crashes into him. Suddenly, he has to vomit. A violent burst. Alberto discharges it on the wall, holding his belly and screaming. His throat is ripped, he discovers, so now gastric stuff and air bubbles between mouth and trachea, just under his chin. He throws up again, hacking. A pinwheel of pain starts spinning from feet to head. His whole body rebels, now. The effort widens a hole in his abdomen, letting intestine prolapse. Alberto must hold his guts in with his hands. Bowels seem pushed out by a centrifuge. An unexplainable taste of moldy potatoes comes up to his nose, then he lets acid and bile out in two regurgitations to join the hot muddle on and around his feet.
A man – face hidden behind his *Corriere dello Sport* newspaper – keeps clear, but he can't avoid nausea. "Ew, holy heaven!"
Alberto keeps leaning with his head against the wall, gasping with rotten breath, all his muscles awakening at the abnormal burning of his flesh.
"I've got rabies. Oh, Jesus, I've got rabies," he mutters, spitting acidic saliva into the vomit puddle. He feels like crying. He's lost his smartphone.

Mom and Dad must be seriously worried.

Last night he went out to listen to some music, for some dancing and tripping, but what happened next is a blank.

Air turns to fire inside his lungs. Sunlight makes the wounds fry all over his body.

Into the shadows, cool, now.

Alberto turns back, his neck covered in gastric fluids, to see how far he had walked from the hospital.

Not so much.

He no longer cares about the ER; now he's interested in the woods surrounding the building.

He runs away as a dog pulls its owner to the puddle he'd left on the sidewalk.

Alberto climbs a pipe, up the hospital compound wall. He reaches the iron fence on top, slides through the bars and then disappears into the trees.

Nobody seems to have seen him. And nobody must see him until the end of the day.

A good rest is necessary to regain his energy.

Once dusk comes, he will think how to go back home. Maybe. The only thing in his mind, now: *the woods.* More so than his home.

Alberto hides in a small area of San Camillo's park. No personnel, no patients, and no cars. A small, overgrown, solitary jungle will be the perfect crib. His stomach finally calms, and the rest of his body seems quieter, too.

Alberto tries to sleep, gasping in the shadow of the bushes, while the sun burns in the sky.

It's sunset when suddenly he wakes after a long, dark and empty slumber. His dry throat cannot let the air through. It's like he had swallowed sand.

The cut on his neck is encrusted.

Water. Need water.

Alberto rises. Every bone screams in pain.

A violent ache from his ears smashes him down again, the sound of movement way too loud.

The boy creeps on dead foliage. The rustle is an unbearable din. Distant cars from the main street, near the hospital entrance, make a deadly noise. Those metal sounds are like little chisels poking at his eardrums. Alberto presses his palms on his ears.

Still. You must stand still.

Still.

All right. Better.

Inside his head, after that lightning bolt of pain, his mind seems to open like a rose, animated by powerful, clear, external signals.

First of all, the noises.

City noises – limpid, huge – begin to reveal themselves, a world never heard before.

Alberto feels like he's fallen deep into reality, where his own breathing is Earth's sonic carpet.

The infinitesimal crackling of plants, trees, crops ... arriving from everywhere. But Nature's speech isn't painful to him.

Still hidden under the bushes, Alberto waits.

Inside every tree and every log, sap flows in an unstoppable suction, while branches snap as though the entire wood around the building were stretching its limbs before falling asleep.

Even from the ground, a moisty whisper.

Alberto can hear all the sounds of the world.

All.

The roots in secular motion, among worms and insects, dwellers of the warm womb of the underground. Coming from the street – from the boiling dry asphalt – Alberto hears a dog breathing; and to the breath of all the dogs inside nearby houses, too, whose senses are triggered by their fellow's passing on the sidewalk. Tree fronds rumble against the gentle breeze. Trees protect the basic actions of scrawny fledglings that scream and ask for food from their nests.

Then the smells arrive.

The dry, stinging stink of a stray cat's spray on the hood of a parked car. Alberto's skin can read several unknown whiffles of life, chemical emanations, floating in the air. He could follow every trace and go back to its origin, but the clash with a primal odor, a basic smell, shocks him and blocks him there in the bushes, making him forget the damn thirst for water scorching him. And the sounds invading his mind.

Blood.

The smell of blood.

Yes, blood.

His skin recognizes it, too.

Blood is more interesting somehow; it's the only thing he wants, now.

More than that, blood has completely hypnotized him.

He must take off those ragged clothes.

He has to free his skin.

His wounds have closed their mouths. But within him is an inexplicable passion. A sort of huge anxiety, a paranoid vortex of unnamed fears.

He wishes to be naked, while the countless sounds of creation keep pouring inside his mind – water from a fountain. He begins to feel that wild symphony of industrial and organic like a shelter, enabling him to blend.

The smell of blood comes from the back of the hospital. Only few steps away. Close.

Must explore.

Naked, he slides along the walls. With every motion, his muscles dart with myoclonic spasms. The more Alberto moves, the stronger he feels. Sound frequencies – high, medium and low – run through his ear canals, chasing him and putting him on alert. His eyes keep everything under control, so Alberto can find a reason for each sound. He could see a single blade of grass shift, now, if he focused, or locate an earthworm or a slug a hundred meters away, but he has no time to practice.

His mind only says *field clear, no danger.* But … *clear of what?*

What if he meets someone? What would he say or do, naked and wounded?

From the self-propelled patchwork of sounds and smells, images begin to take shape: crickets, worms, leaves, maggots, cars, birds, lizards. The magma of external signals generates specific visualizations, which is why it also neutralizes the stream of thought-words – increasingly useless and senseless.

His mind decomposes language structures and begins to work only through images. This happens automatically, and Alberto doesn't notice.

He tries to say: *Oh, my God, what am I doing here?* but what comes out of his cut throat is a choppy gasp. At the same time, a searing pain spears his forehead and brain.

A flame of color bursts in the gloom of his shut eyes, until his senses focus on the olfactory cloud of blood.

There, a little window at the foot of the wall, spreading out that plasma breath.

No one around.

Alberto leans down and takes a look. Impossible to see inside; there's a thick metal screen. Entering the place isn't going to be an issue. Somewhere, there's a door.

Gallons of blood are calling him without a reason. Alberto stands and moves away, looking for a door, sheltered by the twilight. Even the building is muttering something with its walls, overburdening its foundations. In the distance, the siren of an ambulance leaving the hospital. A dog barks, annoyed by that violent, unnatural and obsessive lament, just like Alberto. His heart beats hard in his chest. Anxiety turns into hatred and rage. He can't take all that noise. His throat burns inside with infinite thirst. Drink. He must drink, quickly.

There, an iron door.

The need for blood runs side by side with the necessity to stay hidden and move unseen.

Sounds of water behind the door, but the door is closed.

Anger rises up from his bowels, up his chest, through his heart, filling his shoulders, biceps, and boiling right into his hands.

Grasp the handle. Twist it. Open the door to reach blood and water.

The iron wrings slowly.

His breath is a living beast and his lungs want oxygen to give his hands the power to crack the iron until the door is open. A guttural roar comes up his throat with the last effort. Alberto opens the door that gives way with a harsh noise.

A wall of warm and stale air runs over him. While dust dances, his eyes scan the darkness of the room. He can see everything. Standing still in the deserted room, with no light, he reads the position of every object and the space through which he could move. Noises of people from remote places reach his consciousness across the concrete and iron of the building, and with the air blowing through the halls. Close to him, there is a sink.

Drink.

Alberto must drink. Making the bone of his hands creak, Alberto grabs the knob and twists. At first, water spews out in dirty gushes, then it flows free and cool. Yearning, Alberto dives in. The fluid goes into his throat, into his nose. He gasps, twitching, then falls on his knees. Almost drowning. He coughs to empty his lungs and nose.

Damn water.

Everything burns within.

Everything burns.

Knocked out by a sip of water from a fucking tap.

Outside, an owl gives a hoot, as though laughing at him. He catches his breath, calms; then, Alberto waits, motionless.

A strange pain penetrates his face.

At first, his nose spills blood and snot; then bones slide on one another with loud creaking. At the center of his skull, between eyes and mouth, his nose seems to widen like shotgun barrels. The smells grow even more in his nostril: dust, flesh, paper, saliva, even of people who passed through this room who knows when; the wood, plastic, iron, rubber, asphalt, urine, feces, plaster, varnish, and finally: *blood*, over them all. The fluid tissue triumphs inside his face, creating a vision of rebirth. His brain works like a cement mixer to figure out the blood he's smelling – a burning spiral – setting mind and muscles on fire.

Blood, yes.

Blood.

There is a lot of human blood, somewhere.

Field clear, no danger.

Alberto steps ahead while his breath becomes short and syncopated.

His face hurts.

Men, far away.

Alberto opens a second door that leads into a sort of pit. It's quite dark because of feeble neon lights. The plaster on the walls is ruined and stained with moisture. There is a stone staircase, then a narrow corridor. And an elevator door. Alberto leans out to peer into the corridor. Nobody in sight. Blood calls from the darkest corner of the corridor. Barefoot, Alberto can run unheard on the cool floor. He passes a shadowy area, the smell of plasma condenses, thickening the air. The corridor ends among old closed doors, windows looking on the woods outside, and a staircase with a wooden handrail going down to the basement. Upstairs, someone is pushing something with small wheels. Alberto sneaks downstairs, fast like a rat, tasting the darkness with his entire skin.

He is on the underground level of the building. A tunnel tiled in white – lined with cables and pipes and buzzing, bubbling tubing – shows a huge carousel of doors and forks. The wiring works badly, and the light comes and goes. The wet air stench of mold and saltpeter. Blood rests inside one of the chambers at the end of the hall. No human sounds. Boilers are working, pumps, accumulators, electric ticking, hisses of water and other unrecognizable noises.

Alberto finds the door of the room with the blood inside.

Not locked, simply ajar.

He steps inside. There is little fresh air.

In the shadows, his eyes take in the room from side to side.

Near the ceiling, he spots the little window he tried to look through while outside. The environment is roomy, full of tables in a chessboard pattern. Sinks at the far end. Drops of water fall into the metal basins with thundering splashes.

A thin noise. Something has moved.

His eyes begin to see clearly in the darkness. His ears pick up movements. The room is crowded by human beings lying on the tables and covered with tarps. Alberto watches their shapes under the shrouds. In the dark, they are infinitely motionless as they sleep their deaths. However, something moves, right under the little window.

Alberto's ear denotes the hidden source of a heartbeat.

He steps back into a corner, beside a locker, to wait and see.

On the table under the window, the shroud rises; then a man – facedown under the tarp – comes out, pushing on his arms, moans, arching his back and shaking his loins against the surface. Alberto's nostrils widen, sensing flesh and blood. As his stomach cramps, he growls softly.

The stranger realizes he's not alone in the room. He freezes. And listens.

Rage, fear, terror.

Alberto doesn't understand. His heart stomps with fury while all senses feel like a discharge of cold shocks from the inside out, piercing his skin. His breath gets shorter, faster. The man hears him breathing; among the bodies, one perceives the presence of the other.

The stranger cannot see in the dark; Alberto knows that.

The man gets down from the table, the shroud falling off him and to the floor.

Alberto now sees the woman once lying under the man. Her belly cut, opened wide with a surgical retractor. She's dead. The living man is naked, muddy with the slurries which came out the dead woman, and his stick-for-breeding is huge and filthy with plasma. Alberto feels the man's heart hammering, his nerves tensing to the breaking point. Maybe he wants to run away. The man knew he would have to move in the dark; he easily finds his clothes under the table, where he had left them before making love with the corpse. Alberto sees him watching at nothingness in the dark while he puts on his long lab coat. His fear yields adrenaline, making his skin give out a stink Alberto cannot tolerate. The corpses' smell is good. The fear is nasty, irritating; it is a wrath trigger. The blood-covered man is dressed, now, so his clothes get drenched. Alberto suddenly pounces. The prey runs among the tables, blindly, toward the door, fear slowing down his thoughts.

Alberto, unseen, gets out of the room first.

He watches the man coming out the door, running through the hall toward the staircase. Alberto lets him flee, but only for a few seconds.

A wake of adrenaline odor has driven Alberto to the prey like a fluorescent wire in the shadows.

The man is showering in the dressing room.

Out of the windows, black clouds blot out the silver eye of the moon.

The water stops flowing.

Alberto waits in the shadows, near the door. Enraged by the stink of fear, still in the air, a pressing desire to slaughter hammers his mind. A mad anguish begins to squeeze his neck more and more.

The man comes out of the shower. He puts on a white robe. He's not stupid at all, and once again he feels there's someone in the dark watching him. This time, he decides to turn on the light and see.

Alberto turns it off using another switch, right beside him.

"Who the fuck are you?" the man asks in a roaring voice.

Fear.

Alberto answers, but his voice is a bray from his cut throat, vocal cords drowned in slime.

At the inhuman sound, the man in the robe sways in confusion. His fear makes him stink again.

Enemy. Danger.

The prey moves toward the windows. Maybe he wants to jump out.

Alberto attacks.

"What –"

Alberto grabs his neck and shoves him down on the floor. Staring at his eyes. His rage is his will and the prey can do nothing against his violent energy.

The moon is free from the clouds, now, and illuminates the room in silver.

The prey looks up at the younger man above him. Now he can see him: disfigured, angry, disoriented. He catches Alberto's wrists and digs his fingertips in his tendons. Alberto immediately loses his grip, then he's unhorsed. The man is stronger; he overpowers the boy, twisting his arm behind his back and knocking him down with his face against the floor.

"Did you think you could fool me?"

Alberto doesn't answer, gasping into the ground.

"What the fuck do you want with me, asshole?" he insists. "So? What the fuck are you looking for? Not talking, eh?" He shakes him, almost breaking his arm.

Alberto stops resisting. The man believes the boy has given up, so he loosens his grip. He stands, letting Alberto turn with his back to the floor. The man pins him down with a foot on his chest. He doesn't recognize him; the boy isn't one of his patients.

Alberto is short of breath. His scarred face is a ruin. He turns his face to the moon.

Its' full.

His eyes widen with horror.

Alberto keeps watching the moon, as though asking it for help or mercy.

The man doesn't understand. He tries to figure out what the boy's expression means.

Alberto opens his mouth wide, as well as his eyes. His pupils become chasms. His chest heaves with quickening breaths, swelling his ribs outward and outward.

The man steps backward, taking his foot off the boy.

Alberto's bones crackle like wood on fire. A heavy bark bursts from his throat.

The man falls to the ground, annihilated. And he can't help but look at him.

Alberto stands, his back to the moon, his features lost within a dark silhouette, but the man on the floor can perfectly see what the hell is going on. Alberto's shoulders rise as his head lowers. Bones and bowels howl, broiling. Muscles harden and flex under his skin, where hair proliferates.

"Christ," the man whispers.

A spreading tremor shakes Alberto's body. The shape-shifting boy growls, and his chirping nose gives off a harsh blow. He's becoming a monolith under the moon.

The thing that used to be Alberto turns around to face the shining satellite in the sky. It reaches out with its long, powerful arms, sparkling with sweat. With a spasm of final changing, the thing takes a full breath before screaming. Its swelling ribcage makes a loud noise of bones, a bundle of whiplashes.

"What … what are you becoming?" the man cries out.

The thing loudly howls and leaps upon its prey.

Its head explodes in midair.

After the Second Night of Full Moon: Sunday, 4ᵗʰ of July

So, finally, a brand new dawn.

Dark Mary has been in her bed for an hour. She lies on her back, eyes wide open on the mute ceiling. Thursday she played at Geronimo's, Friday at the Alpheus, and Saturday at the Radio Rock Boat, closing her show at 4 a.m. She came home driving her old blue Volkswagen Polo, and put David the snake back inside its terrarium. She took off her red contact lenses. She dropped on her Ikea bed, 4:30 a.m. and still dressed, gingerly laying her nape on the pillow for a pressing cervical ache. Maybe the blame is David's, with its warm-sucking spires creeping around Mary's neck so many hours, despite its precious function of keeping molesters away.

The girl has closed her eyes, a teardrop rolling down, her temples pulsating hard, her ears ringing with a sharp white noise like an out-of-tune TV. Struggling to fall asleep, her mind has found a grim dam: Martyna's presence, growing bulkier. It isn't possible to sleep, with a heart full of anguish. No longer. Not possible. In her sleep, Mary's senses pick up Martyna's oppressive closeness. The woman lies naked, staring at her in the dark. She loves her with that gaze, devours her with her misshapen obsession in a carnivorous desire of possessing, controlling, and manipulating her, following every step she takes, mindreading her thoughts through the movements of her eyes and the direction of her glances. Martyna digests her in silence deep inside her mind.

There was a time when all that felt like a form of adoration. Feeling worshiped was fun, exciting. Martyna got hold of Mary's ego. Then, lost under her rule, Mary realized she'd fallen in a trap, too late. She suddenly knew how hard it would be to break free.

Martyna delves into her, studies her. She counts every single

breath she takes, decoding emotional waves, sifting truth and lies –
like a gold seeker – in every word Mary says.

Martyna is horny, now. She decides to undress Mary, to creep
upon her cold, smooth skin. "You piece of shit," she whispers in her
bad Italian-American accent, licking Mary's earlobe, "you never play
Kiss's 'Betrayed' for me, at your fucking shows."

"That song has fuck to do with the set. Told you a million
times," Mary hisses, ungluing her dry lips.

Martyna is astonished. She thought Mary was asleep. This forces
her, after a pause, to go on with her effusions.

"I need to rest," Mary begs. Her lover stinks of sweat.

"Again? You never get enough," Martyna says.

"Honey, it's almost dawn. I need to sleep," Mary says,
absentmindedly kissing her before turning on her back again, with
no energy left at all.

Martyna doesn't relent. She stubbornly covers her with kisses,
despite Mary saying *Honey* instead of *Love*.

Dark Mary cries a tear, and Martyna sees it. Unmoved with pity,
she goes on after spitting her venomous disapproval: "Cut it out,
you depressed fuck!"

"Please, Marty. I can't."

"Shut up, darling. Don't move."

Martyna's tongue moves like a hysterical, inexperienced slug.
There's nothing good in its wasted, slobbering dance; no reaction
at all in Mary. Wishing to make her lover happy, and to steal a grain
of affection, Martyna keeps doing things her way. It's an effort
borne of pure selfishness. Martyna spreads Mary's legs and dives
her mouth where her loved one wouldn't want her – she hasn't
even washed before going to bed. The smell doesn't stop Martyna.
She hopes to give Mary an orgasm, and then to drink a drop of her
satisfaction from the middle of her legs. DMj undergoes the assault
with loathing, while the air out of her lover's mouth freezes
between her pubis and anus, into a puddle of saliva.

Only in her brain does she take pleasure.

Finally, she falls asleep.

ELSEWHERE ...

Carabinieri ex-Marshal Alfredo Vanacura has a big issue.

It's seven in the morning. For the third time in a month, he's in front of a young body whose head has exploded, the rest of the body a masterpiece of gashes and bites.

Alfredo remembers that sudden call, thirty days ago, when his quiet life was becoming too boring.

"Good evening, Marshal, it's the Prefect. So, how's retirement?"

"Good evening, Mr. Pecoraro. Well, I'm finally catching up with my reading list, I guess. To what do I owe the pleasure?"

"Well, Marshal ... we have a case. One of the strange ones. You know."

"The ones you call me for."

"Yes."

"A good reason to feel less useless, I hope."

"I hope we can leave you back to your retirement soon, Marshal, instead. Maybe."

"I love that maybe."

And here he is now, semi-officially back on the job, a month later. And at the end of his wits.

"He wasn't a patient here, I guess," Alfredo says to San Camillo-Forlanini Hospital's head physician, Giorgi. Alfredo doesn't really seem to expect an answer.

"All our patients are accounted for," Giorgi answers. "This boy must have come from outside."

Alfredo glances at his friend, Max Fildor, the pathologist working on this case. "Just like the last two," he says.

"The last two what?" Giorgi nervously asks.

Alfredo is sensible enough not to answer, silencing any further questions. "Bring it to the morgue," he orders.

"Ours," Fildor clarifies to the head physician, who suddenly looks pale.

Carabinieri RIS Sergeant Marazzi chimes in, "Marshal, we have found the boy's clothes in the woods. In the park behind the hospital."

"Good," Alfredo says, "let's try to –"

"He entered the building by prying open a disused back door. He left footprints of dirt everywhere. They led us to the basement, and from there to the dissection room. I've already sent −"

"I was about to say that," Alfredo grunts.

"I apologize, Marshal," Marazzi says.

"Never mind. Mister Giorgi," Alfredo addresses the head physician, "I need you to come with me to the station. Just for a deposition, of course."

The doctor's face looks worried. Alfredo notices that, and goes on talking. "Take it easy. Official procedures. I know you're not a murderer, but I'd like you to explain to me why this body scares you so much." The ex-Marshal reads in the man's eyes things that want to be told. "You're looking at it as if it could stand up any minute now."

Giorgi is about say something, but Vanacura gives him no time.

"I guess you've seen tons of bodies. Am I right?" he presses. "Bodies, people opened up, freaks … shit, this is the San Camillo!"

After long consideration, the head physician mutters something in a low voice. He looks like he's saying his last wish. "Would you let me go to the bathroom? I only need five minutes. I'm taking laxatives."

"Okay," Alfredo says, annoyed. "Five minutes. No more, though, I still haven't had breakfast."

Meanwhile, Fildor is plumbing the dead's head with his Parker satin-silver fountain pen. Until he finds what he was looking for. Validation analogies.

Alfredo looks at him, wondering why his friend is again using that silver pen. That hunch makes his pineal gland itch.

Fildor is making connections with the last two bodies of that weird case.

Priscilla, twenty-four years old; Roberto, twenty-five. More than a dozen drill holes in the skulls. As if the brain matter suddenly, unexplainably, puffed up, until bursting the skull – compromised by those holes – and exploding all around, Fildor sums in his mind, discovering the first drill hole under the body's hair.

Giorgi is still using the bathroom. The pathologist stands, nodding to the RSI agents and signaling them to take a photographic report of the scene before bagging the corpse. "From this angle first. Then, from the bathroom door. I want a ton of pics, all the patterns of blood and brain spatter … walls, floor, ceiling. Take a photo of every single shred of grey matter that flew on the ground. Oh, and the floor must be covered with prints of bare feet; make sure you don't miss them."

Alfredo takes a look at his watch. Twelve minutes. He says, annoyed at the agent next to the door. "Please, knock hard for our friend."

The guard knocks, calls Mr. Giorgi. No answer. The guard knocks again, and calls louder. Then he turns to his Marshal. The hospital is surrounded by policemen – the man in the bathroom cannot have escaped. Alfredo hurries in to pry open the door.

"Holy shit," the agent whispers.

Giorgi hasn't fled through the window, but away from something he could no longer hide. Hanging from the ceiling with a robe belt around his neck, his eyes – open wide – stare at the Marshal, as though waiting just for him. As a physician, he well knew how to die strangled fast with a good knot.

Alfredo's first thought, in front of the swinging body with its feet dripping urine, is Mr. Giorgi's panicked expression when Fildor mentioned the dissection room. "Okay. Let's go and see what the hanged dude was hiding."

Perfectly in sync with Alfredo's plans, Sergeant Marazzi comes back into the dressing room as the head-exploded corpse is bagged and lifted. "Marshal," he says in a smug voice. "Please, come down to the dissection room."

Alfredo is getting pissed off. He's unfairly bothered by worthy Marazzi's perfect timing – the Sergeant's only and ugly fault is saying or doing the things other people are thinking. Marazzi is a true, beloved pro, but he doesn't realize he's crossing the boundless minefields of Alfredo's insecurities. "Fildor," Alfredo says, before the Sergeant can add even further exciting deductions. "Let's take down Mr. Giorgi and search the shower room from top to bottom."

The pathologist puts back the silver pen in his pocket and enters the bathroom, toward the still-warm body.

"What a shitty Sunday," Alfredo mutters. "All we need is Mom overcooking my linguine."

THIRD NIGHT OF FULL MOON: SUNDAY, 4ᵀᴴ OF JULY

Bodies are pretty to look at.

They sleep the sweetness of the eternity. To them, life has been a one-act play of events, a linear drama stretching toward the roof of existence. The corpse is the mask the actor takes off. And, as we can never know who a person really is, the truth behind a man's mask dissipates in his last breath. And then the soul shifts into an inconceivable place human senses cannot reach. All we have left is the corpse, the body, which is like an empty, abandoned house. If a human essence used to live within it, now it contains the space of an unholy cathedral, where strange sounds from nowhere make majestic echoes. A dead body is ready for anything. A human being is not. The creases on the skin of a naked corpse write a dramatic dynamism; while during life, they are details nobody looks at and neither sees. Bodies own a royal, sexless sensuality: disarmed of moral-based restriction, all mind-barriers zeroed, flesh becoming the real essence, the heavenly land for the bravest adventurers.

Martyna photographs corpses.

She's the webmaster of decoroner.net, where her digital pictures float, edited with Photoshop filters and brushes. The pics are taken using a Sony DSLRA900, 24.6 megapixels, Nex5HB telephoto lens, and they build galleries of anonymous models offering all their involuntary plastic art to the world's eyes.

Inspired by both compatriot Joel Peter Witkin's art, and the world-wide success of rotten.com, Martyna follows in the steps of corpse art; she explores morgues and their mute population, at hospitals and university forensics classes, where nameless cold people wait – with no line – for surgical tools.

Her pictures brought legal action and impounding death threats and excommunications because they revealed every secret about the naked nature of the dead. The wrecking of a skull, the section of an arm, the deadly work of a weapon, the weirdest mutilations.

The cobweb of veins, the cyanotic swamps of flesh next to decay – flesh wounded by accidents or murderous hand.

To Martyna's camera, all that – and more – becomes an earthly garden of dangerous seductive power. As the motion picture of life has completely bled out from a person, each opening of a corpse sings a hypnotic rhapsody. A poem of aseptic virginity. Flesh can give shape to great sculptures. Rose-shaped ulcerations by electric shock or bullets, eyelet-shaped slashes typical of blades, erosion craters from a fire. Cadaveric skin can compose the horizon of a silent gaseous planet, with all the colors and slinky forms of atmospheric turmoil. The stains of static blood shine with dark light as nightly oases. Venous and arterial ramifications, darkening under the skin, paint branches with no leaves, almost like fire-tattoos.

The initial repulsion completely transforms the observer, grabbing his soul and carrying him into an alien autumn of ecstatic madness.

A dead person possesses the charm of a movie relic. A scenography, a costume, an animatronic dummy, a spaceship diorama. To destroy the magic of a motion picture, all you have to do is show its tricks. And, as photography freezes the race of time, turning it into death, then photo-shooting the dead can kill the fear of the living, once and for all.

Looking at the pictures of the dead, the novice could feel pain because in doing that he's burying his fear under the foundations of his soul, cutting off the most sensitive limb of his emotional range. It is like a mournful loss, Stendhal's syndrome, sensory standby – until pleasure surprisingly comes.

Born in New York, March 21st, 1980, at 4:45, her father was from Italy; Martyna attends the Art Institute on Varick Street. Aged twenty, she drops out to follow an older guy named Matthew, a guitarist from San Francisco. Alcohol virtuoso, Satanist, Matt is hooked on tombs and corpses. His addiction has developed at his father's funeral home, Nelson's FH, where he works cleaning, shaving, and dressing the dead.

In that mortuary, for starters, Martyna loses her cherry – raped and beaten by Matt. After that, he locks her inside the lab for a whole weekend together with the corpses. It is Martyna's initiation, necessary baptism for a journey of love beyond conformism. During these two days, Matt does a couple of gigs in Manhattan with his tribute band, Dead Jesus, playing songs by Obituary, Morbid Angel, Misfits, Type 0 Negative, Necromance, and Bathory.

Back home, Monday morning at dawn, Matt finds Martyna in deep catatonic state. He takes his amp and guitar out of his Ford Gran Torino, then puts Martyna inside the trunk. He drinks some beer, then starts toward Sproul State Forest, Pennsylvania. He wants to leave his girlfriend in his mad friend Gohen's capable hands. Gohen is from Scandinavia, and he lives in a squat in those woods. He's turned the dining room into a sanctuary for sacrifices, and that's the perfect place for Matt to reanimate Martyna with some amphetamines and porno-esoteric rituals, all to go down while he's away.

Thursday, Matt comes back to take his girlfriend home. Gohen hasn't called him. Matt knocks at the Scandinavian's door, but it goes down like cardboard. So he enters. It seems like entering into the album cover of *Symphonies of Sickness* by his favorite band, Carcass. He can't make out his friend Gohen's features from the other guys, probably mustered for the party with little Martyna, because of a sea of clotty blood covering everything and leaking from the ceiling. But there's something more than blood. Matt begins to tremble. In that red glue, he can spot tracks of bears and wolves, drawn by the crushing odor. There is no surface free from pieces of flesh. Limbs and bowels ripped off, slashed, and thrown everywhere by an unimaginable fury.

Where is she in that massacre?

Matt realizes he has only ever played like a kid with corpses, with his prudish necrophilia. This slaughter is simply too much for him. He's about to lose what little sense he has left. This is total apocalypse. More than swallowing Jack Daniel's with lysergic acid.

What about his affairs with the dead, his pathetic anarchy, his heavy metal proselytism now?

Everything comes crashing down like the walls of Jericho, now that Death does its frontal assault. It just takes seconds and Matt is a child again, with a simple mind; he almost cries, beginning to faint, far as he feels now from his miserable adulthood and his ludicrous evil – in the presence of the work of a *real* beast.

Matthew's fear, though buried under the choking stink of slaughter, alerts the sense of smell of someone hiding nearby in the shadows of the forest. Someone screams, beginning to chase him. Matt tries to run away, until his cirrhotic liver bursts, making him collapse facedown into the ground.

Jaws fall on his back, grinding him with bites from his butt to his neck. Buttock and leg flesh is torn off his bones, his back muscles ripped from his ribs. His awareness turns off among blood and vomit and a choppy prayer to God.

"You're putting makeup on me without looking," Dark Mary says. "Where are you, Martyna?"

"Thinking about my pics," she lies, her memories cut short by her girlfriend. She's straddling Mary on her thighs. Her beloved deejay doesn't wear her red lenses, and David lazily moves in its terrarium. Martyna handles the eyeliner with some difficulty; she's getting nervous.

"You're thinking about your pics," Mary insists. "The pics you've taken?"

"I had a good idea," Martyna whispers, breathing a calcified aroma in Mary's face.

"What kind of good idea? Tell me."

"An idea for my photos, Mary. What else? I had a new idea for some new photos. And what about you? Have you got a new DJ set?"

"I've asked what are you thinking about, and you don't answer. You're so mean tonight, really."

"As you always are," Martyna replies in a low, firm voice while sharpening the eyeliner pencil. "To me."

"I hate you," Mary confesses, without any particular inflexion.

"At least, that's a feeling. Dear fucking-record-tinkerer of mine. Where are you going to work tonight? What sort of boring track list did you set up?"

"I'm not going out for work, tonight. There's a birthday party at Goa's. Dario Argento's daughter, Asia. The manager invited me."

Mary pauses. "You knew that. You said you didn't want to go with me. As you can see, I'm going anyway."

"When I declined, I was hoping you did the same to stay with me. That just proves what I suspected: you want to fuck Asia. Nothing more than public relations, right? You want to hook up with her and leave me."

"You're paranoid. There's a Radio Rock DJ, a friend of mine, who's playing for her. So I'm going to listen to some music."

"Oh, no. Bullshit. I think you simply ... yes, goddamn, you hope Asia will be impressed by you, then the two of you get along, then you fuck her because she makes you so horny. So she will bring you in, into the loop, you know? Maybe you'll make a movie, right, and then bye-bye Martyna."

"I'm going at Goa's because – guess what? – that's part of my job. I want to listen to the music played by a DJ at a VIP party. It's my duty and my right to know what's going on in town. And to be seen around. Since I'm popular, just like them."

"You're a disgusting whore."

"And if I make friends with Asia, or someone else, maybe something new will happen. I love my job."

"You love blowjobs."

"Stop it, asshole."

"So, it's clear: you and Asia are friends already. You're calling her by her first name. Yeah, very good."

"Are you drunk, Marty? Did you do Red Bull and coke again? Give me an answer. Did you do Red Bull and coke again?"

"You're a bitch. All you think about is selling yourself out. You are living marketing."

"Finish my makeup, please. It's getting late."

"You're a fuckin' bitch. You're looking forward to spreading your legs and letting some sad, depressed, obese dyke eat you out."

"Take your hands off my face. You're completely insane today."

"Do you want Asia Argento to eat you out in the Goa's toilet, or in the parking lot. I'm warning you: I know all the dark corners around Goa's. I can come, check everywhere."

"Thank you for informing me about that. So, I'd better find another place for fucking, just in case."

"Then it's true."

"Fix me a White Russian, if you can. You're sick."

"No, I'm not. I'm being realistic, instead. I've got the password to your Myspace account. I've read everything – all those men and women who want to fuck you. I'm not paranoid; I'm in love with you, and jealous. Because you provoke people. You'd wink at anybody only to humiliate me."

"Do as you please, Martyna," Mary whispers. The she blurts out, "At least I'm doing something to make this time less of a shit!" She moves away from Martyna, picking up her Hello Kitty purse from the table. She turns her back to him. Wrong move. Her girlfriend sneaks up from behind her and hugs Mary. With rage. Her arms are so powerful. Mary cannot breathe. She fights in vain as Martyna pulls her down on the floor backward, upon her. "Can't you see how fragile you are, little slut? Now it's my turn. You're not going anywhere; you're staying here to make love with me."

"Let's see about that," Mary growls, digging her nails deep in Martyna's thighs.

Her girlfriend lets go, holding back a scream. The wounds slowly spit blood.

Mary turns around in a flash, overpowering the woman with her back still to the floor. She grips Martyna's neck with a hand. Then, aims her nails at her ice-blue eyes. "I'll cut your eyeballs and slurp the vitreous inside. Maybe then you'll give up always watching me. Then I'll rip out your tongue and make you eat it roasted. So maybe you'll give up wearing me out with your hysterical bullshit."

Martyna trembles. Anger is about to explode, but she senses that her Dark Mary is not kidding at all. Her eyes begin to come out of their sockets, her temples swelling like pipes under her skin, turning to purple. Her pretty face changes into something horrible.

She's been keeping Mary under such pressure for so long that the DJ could *really* pluck out her eyes. Cowardly, Martyna order her eyes to shed a tear.

DMj caves in, in front of someone crying.

"Please, Mary, don't do it," Martyna moans, resting her head on the floor. She doesn't care about the slashes on her legs anymore. Not even about the spilling blood. "I beg you."

Dark Mary swallows. She wasn't ready for tears. "Martyna, you're so mean. This is not love, but mind-torture," she says. "Do we *have* to torment each other? Why? Why do you read my private messages? I'd never do that with your account," she whispers, taking her hand off Martyna's neck.

"I didn't only read them. I've even answered, and then deleted everything. Using your account," Martyna explains, "they thought they were talking to you. I played along with those who want to fuck you … so there are a lot of people now, waiting for a private date with Dark Mary."

Mary isn't surprised at all. "Maybe it's *you* who'd like to fuck them," she asks, rising to her feet, staring at her girlfriend's eyes. Time to get out, dispensing with both red lenses and David. It's late. "Staying in the loop is a part of success. If your photos can't give you that, it's not my fault. You can't be angry with me."

"Where are you going now?"

"To the party. At Goa's. How many times do I have to tell you?"

Martyna pretends to cry, sitting on the floor. She hides her face in her hands, her back and shoulder bones loudly creaking.

"See you tomorrow morning, Martyna," Mary says, opening the door. "But if you don't see me back home, that'll be thanks to your genius; maybe I'll be screwing one or more of my Myspace friends I'm going to meet soon. So, my dear depressing bipolar fuck, you can start crying for real now. The more, the better. Goodbye."

Mary closes the door.

She won't see what's about to happen.

VERNISSAGE: WEDNESDAY, 7TH OF JULY

Half-past 9 p.m. Jewish Ghetto, Costaguti Square.

Marshal Vanacura is at his private office, a sixty-square-meter studio flat. A small dining room, where an old bench is buried under books; two bookcases in dark mahogany wood dating back to the sixties, both full, rising from a wooden floor covered with books; a leather chair overloaded with books. There is a little bathroom with no window. The entrance is a short hall cheered up by a coat-rack cabinet fitted with a large mirror, shelf, and Japanese ornaments.

Alfredo is preparing his Savinelli pipe, Deco model, Virginia Gordon Pym tobacco, Original Golden Yellow series. A good smoke is an essential key to shed light over a mass of doubts when he is on one of his peculiar detections. Sometimes.

On the free area of the old bench, several photos are scattered: murdered bodies attached to their corresponding forensic dossiers, all signed by Fildor. The case has been ironically named *Scanners.*

Within a month, three people aged between twenty and thirty-five have been dismembered and eaten alive in Rome.

The anthropophagic killer acts by night. He chases or forces his victims toward marshy or isolated places. Up to now, he seems to favor the Tiber's and Aniene's banks, where he can butcher his prey. Once they're dead, he brings them elsewhere, careful not to leave any trace.

But is this really a man, devouring his victims like that?

Considering the conditions of the bodies, the Marshal is brought to think that maybe the killer doesn't act alone. He could be ordering an animal to thrash his victims after the murder. An attack dog the size of a Rottweiler, or even a wild beast like a hyena, according to the teeth marks on the corpses. Instead, the claw marks – jagged lacerations made by blunt nails – don't match with canine prowlers, being more similar to a bear's. These slashes are four to six inches deep, and the confusing marks on the ground would seem to confirm the bear theory.

But, of course, it would be very difficult to manage a predator that size in a city.

If there's anything true about this lead, the killer could be some kind of circus worker, a tamer of wild beasts. Male, probably. Slender enough not to leave footprints. Below 120 pounds. Possibly Russian or gipsy. He could have mastered a small grizzly bear, about 180 pounds, unleashing it against the victim. Then, he could have ordered the beast to stand aside for him – somehow managing to stop its bloody feast – to step in and drill the victim's skull.

"But what about the issue of the exploding heads?" Alfredo whispers to himself. "Why does that happen days after their deaths?" He blows smoke and questions out the window. Then his mind goes to the organic traces left by the killer, sampled from the wounds. "And what sense does it make that his DNA spontaneously changes some of its nitrogen compounds?"

Priscilla was found with her head exploded on the Casilina Ringroad bypass on the 3rd of June, under a railway underpass, Ettore Fieramosca Street. The lethal wounds on her body dated her death to May 26th; the skull explosion to June, 2nd. No doubt, there's a strange inconsistency. No trace of explosive device placed inside the head by the assassin.

"That's why we can maintain that cause of the explosion is the sudden swelling of the brain ...." Alfredo muses.

So, logically, Priscilla is attacked by the murderer and slashed to death. Then, he drags her body elsewhere, where he can dump it and run away. But there are no traces of wheels or shoes. Not a single one. Then, illogically, Priscilla stands after death, wanders the city alone and unnoticed for a week in a state of total confusion. She holds her bowels in her belly, opened by sixteen claw wounds, her left breast and all major muscles – neck, trapezia, thighs, arms – mutilated. Everything bitten off.

The Carabinieri RIS, thanks to Fildor's autopsy, ascertain that Priscilla walks alone after death, until her head explodes on the 2nd of June, at night. It deflagrates under skin, thanks to the skull-drilling made by the assassin the night of the assault – the night she was slashed and mauled. The mud found in the young victim's mouth, ears, and wounds comes from the Aniene's banks. The dirt entered the cuts during the struggle. Traces of a chase end at a woody river bend, hidden from sight, between outskirt streets of Nomentana and Pietralata. Priscilla was caught among the trees, then beaten, falling on dirt and grass. The assassin and his beast overwhelm the girl, who tries to fight back – presumably scratching the animal's legs. The hunting ground has registered and preserved all the marks of the assault, including partial blood spatter. The skull piercings are done after the butchery using a 9-millimeter self-powered drill. Two occipital holes, two parietal, two temporal.

"I guess," Alfredo whispers, stepping back from the window and handling his smoking pipe, "the killer, or an accomplice, already knows the victim will rise after death. But they can't keep the victims home to kill them a second time. The drill holes must be done so the dead can die later by themselves, elsewhere, alone. The killer knows his victim will rise again – but he wants to stop them. Who knows why …?"

Priscilla is the first one.

Roberto is the second.

He is found three days after his head exploded, which happened the 2nd of June as well. Close to Appian Way, out of Rome, on the overgrown fields of Divino Amore. The young man was 180 pounds, six feet tall. He could have fought back the attacker and his beast. But the fierce animal probably knocked him out right away, snapping and thrashing his throat. Roberto's neck was stripped to his vertebrae. Then, the beast ate his chest and legs.

"Does the killer eat human flesh himself?" the Marshal mutters.

On the rest of Roberto's body, the beast had its fun tearing his flesh. It is clear that, in that location, they took their time.

Even in Roberto's case, the drill holes – made about one hour after his death – let the swelling brain burst the skull. This time, two days later. Roberto was attacked by the beast on the 31st of May. Roberto didn't walk away from the crime scene as Priscilla had. He remained there, unreasonably, until his head exploded.

Alberto is the latest. Third *Scanners* case. Modality of death similar to the predecessors. Assault and explosion within a few hours – this is the only difference. Alberto has the strength and will to reach a hospital, walking far away from the place of attack.

"Ironically," Alfredo says, smiling and blowing out smoke clouds, "Alberto lets us unmask a necrophiliac head physician, who kills himself. Could he be an accessory? Mr. Giorgi was a doctor, he could be the driller killer. He *had* the funny little habit of sexually desecrating female corpses in the hospital mortuary."

Does the murderer choose his victims at random?

"The drilling of the skull is the true serial signature in these killings," Alfredo says to himself, musing.

It shows an objective: helping the swelling brain to burst the skull of the reanimated victim.

It is not natural for human brains to spontaneously grow. Some forms of tumor, or internal bleeding, could do that.

"And even allowing for the living-dead" – the Marshal is an open-minded man who has seen some weird stuff – "aren't you supposed to shoot them in the head? Why doesn't the killer just smash their head right away?"

The puzzle doesn't seem to offer elements the Marshal can put together into any acceptable framework.

Alfredo blows sweet smoke away, staring at the closed rolling shutters of the window in front of him. An old attic that has been empty for years.

"That damn window. It makes my pineal gland itch."

Father Sebastiano, the pale-skinned priest, would like to go out. But he has to surrender to one of his terrible respiratory crises. He's home, now, coughing into the sink that black stuff that comes out of his lungs. A sort of clay, mixed with snot, forming in his chest every time he administers last rites. Maybe the strange matter is like a guano of sins dying men leave inside him. And it makes the priest's porphyria worse, forcing him to hide away from sun and lights.

His skin is white ivory, thickening in a tangle of veins on his chest, neck and face, as the strain to cough out the clay grows harsh and violent. His clear blue eyes, almost as transparent as glass, show red streaks that make him look like a ghost.

"Good God, why do you do this to me?" he whispers, leaning on the sink, slobbering long threads.

Sebastiano won't officiate Vespers tonight. He can't. His cough sounds like death rattles in a cave, the consequence of a deep, long slumber. During which, the black clay from the lungs sedimented.

He tried to kill himself to escape his curse, but something went wrong and he failed to die. He only slept a strange death, a gentle collapse of some hours, during which he saw his life flowing through his eyes. He had found shelter in a hidden ditch in the park of Villa Torlonia, a place where he could disappear. There, he cut the veins of his arms and fell asleep. Then, the following dusk, he awoke alive, but feeling a sense of loss. During his deadly rest, the clay from the lungs settled, proliferating with its taste of dry ink, coming up to the priest's throat in a burning bolus of regurgitation.

"Sebastiano. Father Sebastiano, please, open the door."

The porphyria-sick priest hears knocking at his door. Someone is calling him. It's Mirella, the old and caring landlady who lives downstairs. Sebastiano's sink works just like a phonograph horn, broadcasting downward all the sounds made by the pale priest as he washes himself, as well as when he throws up. He'd better go and open the door; he doesn't want to alarm his neighbor.

"Good evening, Mrs. Mirella. I beg your pardon, I must have been noisy," Sebastiano says in a thin, grating voice.

"Oh, Father. I'm so sorry," the lady says, with her hands on her mouth. "Are you feeling all right? Do you need something? Your face looks so tired …."

"Please, come in. I was preparing to go out."

Mirella enters the dark of Sebastiano's home. She knows the flat; she owns it. It's easy for her to move in there, even with no light. She also knows her tenant needs to protect himself against sunrays, keeping down the blinds and covering the windows with heavy curtains.

"This cough is a curse, ma'am. Do you have any suggestion?"

Mirella has her answer at the ready: "I guess a good herbal tea – mauve leaves and cloves – should be good for you, Father. Or the thermal baths, of course." Mirella walks down the hall, softly lit by a couple of candles. "Isn't it Vespers hour? They must be waiting for you in church."

From a door left ajar, a little lamp radiates its light, offering a few details of a room. Mirella is drawn to it by something – a presence – waiting for a visit, spreading its subtle call of dirt and mold, and a soft chatter, almost imperceptible.

Sebastiano is in the bathroom, washing; Mirella moves closer to the dim room. Through the crack between door and frame, in the shadows, she glimpses a slice of the old damask wallpaper she chose back in 1965, and of the Swedish TV cabinet – nothing else.

Mirella doesn't see who's sitting on the red chair against the wall, facing the door.

The old lady softly lays her hand on the doorknob, hesitating.

Inside, head and shoulders draped in shadows, a woman sits in silence. Mirella cannot see her black-skinned hands on the red armrests, her red plaid skirt. Mirella's hand quivers as, inside, the stranger gives birth to a mass of minced meat out of her open-wide legs. With a low farrowing noise, the motionless sitting woman delivers a blood sausage, dropping it on the floor. A freakish tonnage of it. From inside her body she squeezes out a casting of greasy, glossy purple meat. Mirella feels a sudden nausea, obliterating her other perceptions. It makes her dizzy, she's going to vomit. She leans to the wall, trying to breathe. The priest, in the bathroom, seems completely unaware. Silently, Mirella steps backward and into the dark hall; then she shakes her head, wrinkles her nose at a smell, and marches toward the door, her hand reaching again for the doorknob. Her heart stomps.

"Mirella, I'm ready," the priest says, appearing from the bathroom. She stops in her tracks, turns. Mirella can barely see him in the shadows: his eyes, his clerical collar and the golden cross, and his long, slim white hands.

"Oh," Mirella says, amazed. "You're so handsome."

Marshal Vanacura is just out of Rome's Grande Raccordo Anulare bypass, on a narrow dirt side road called Catena Street. A truck driver has called the Carabinieri, and is gone before their arrival. The patrol has discovered two corpses hidden in the tall grass beside the main road.

It's half past four in the morning when Alfredo arrives. No matches with the *Scanners* case, besides the age of the victims and the weird cause of death. They are both about twenty-five, probably strangers. From their looks, they could be English, German, from Eastern Europe, or from the USA. Both fair-skinned and solidly built. Brothers, maybe, considering their remarkable resemblance to one another. They have no documents, no wallets. Their chests have been skillfully opened – a horizontal cut along the diaphragm.

The corpses could have been spotted only by the high position of a truck cab.

"Where did these poor devils' blood end up?" Fildor asks himself. The bodies lie there, clean cuts to the throats, abdomens slashed. They should float on a lake of blood, about ten liters of red. But the grass is only wet with dew. Those massive wounds are dry. "It looks like, before cutting them up, the killer has completely bled them out," Fildor says, considering. "But how's that possible? Even a physician couldn't make such a clean job. Unless he carries along some kind of suction machine."

The GIP – Preliminary Investigation Judge – won't have any of that. He's in a hurry to go on holiday to Sardinia, where his wife has been waiting for him for a week and she's already pretty pissed off. "Marshal, do me a favor and deal with this felony for me. I know you're investigating some weird shit."

"Yes, but –" Alfredo says.

"This is some weird shit as well," the GIP interrupts. "Weird like you, dear Marshal. Sort this in your case. I've already warned the Prefect. And good luck." He gets back to his black Mercedes, pulled at the roadside, direction city center.

Alfredo's mobile rings as he, offended and thrown, keeps watching at the judge's back. "Hello?" he answers quietly, leaning over the corpses with the first light of dawn while Fildor speaks to the Mortuary agents. "Affirmative, sir. At noon," Alfredo says, hanging up.

"Who was it?" Fildor asks. "If you have to go, I'm warning you: with these two, we already have a full day."

"Prefect."

"Really? Pecoraro called you? What does he want?"

"He asked me if, and when, I'm having lunch."

"And what did you tell him?"

"That I lunch at noon."

"Shut up, jerk. It was your mother," Fildor says, teasing.

"No, it was him. I'm going to meet him, but I told him I can't stay for lunch because I have a prior commitment."

"You really feel like screwing around this morning."

"Why? Wouldn't you lie to anyone for a dish of *spaghetti alla puttanesca?* See you later, mate."

What does the human heart taste like?

Enjoying a dead nectar counts for nothing.

The secret of a human being flows until it is a prisoner inside the holy darkness of flesh. It's quite like water and a bit of sugar, with a preponderant flavor of iron nails and hot unleavened bread, a pinch of salt, some sour butter. Such is its taste while bitten as it still pulsates in the chest. One bite to life, and one to death.

Father Sebastiano coughs the damn black shining mass out of his chest. Does that grainy snot contain his heart? Every time he swallows the soul of someone dying, during last rites, a mass grows inside him. But do their swallowed souls go back to the world when he hacks out the stuff?

Tonight, he has drunk Carlo's essence, one of the faithful of his parish.

Carlo's family called the priest as soon as the doctor said he was about to pass away.

"I am the liver of my flock," Sebastiano said. "I filter its blood. I purify it. I contain the scum that my lambs have accumulated in life, step by step. This is my earthly glory. Do you want to repent of your sins, son?"

"Yes, I do, Father," Carlo muttered. His voice was low as the lights inside his room. Standing apart, his relatives watched Death's arrival, both frightened and excited. They waited for the event. They almost hoped to see, coming off the shadows on the wall, a hooded skeleton in black robe riding a white horse, a scythe held in its boney hands.

Sebastiano took the dying man's confession, holding his powerless hand; he made him talk with his toothless mouth. His sins came out in humble order, with just enough voice to be heard. The confession was cut short in the thick of it. Nobody knew which kind of burden remained unsaid, as Death came unseen. Carlo's soul ran out from his hand into Sebastiano's. The priest felt that warm, spiritual breath across his palm, wrist, tendons, bones, and up the muscles of his arm. It always happens. The soul shifts inside

Sebastiano as the person passes away. From hand to hand. The soul of the dying pours inside Sebastiano as though injected with a syringe, and it wades through his flesh finding no resistance. A soft foam penetrating the Father's body until it finds a place in his chest. At first, the pale priest feels an internal bustle, like a buzzing wasps' nest enclosed inside his ribcage. Then, he senses the dull weight of apparent stasis.

The spreading dark nectar, in which heart and lungs of the sick priest drown, is the digestive residue of what Carlo – and all the others blessed by Sebastiano – should have given back to God. The drainage, cyclically and painfully vomited by Sebastiano, is also the ultimate heart filtration of which he needs to feed. He steals to men what belongs to God. It's his curse, a guilt he's not able to expiate. A physiology perfectly matching his chronic porphyria, a sort of spiritual hunger to which he must obey, eating souls he sucks out of those about to die. He well knows he's a monster, a leech, a parasite no heavenly or infernal sphere will ever host, since death isn't a possible escape route from his freak nature. Call it power. It's his fire within, a flame that neither burns nor dies out. But it always must be cooled. With the coolness of the dying souls.

The sun is rising, so it's easier for Dark Mary to enter the church of San Luigi dei Francesi near Navona Square. Nobody inside the church sees her disappearing in the shadows, between the great light shafts from the windows. Nobody sees her moving through pews and kneelers until she vanishes as a shadow with no body at all.

Sebastiano is inside the vestry. He's collecting in a cup what he suddenly had to cough out. And when his ears stop rumbling, after the fit, the priest seems to hear a steady, soggy thud coming from the nave – a slow shuffling, growing clearer.

A dull clomping of wet cloth.

A mechanical, monotonous drum with a head of wool.

A mallet of soaked hair knocking at a wooden door.

Father Sebastiano knows about it. The church is desert, but it's full of life. More than when it gathers the faithful.

Inside Prefect Giuseppe Pecoraro's office, Alfredo sits, waiting to stand.

"Are you all right, Marshal?"

"Yes. Thank you, Mr. Prefect. I was wondering."

"A coffee, before you go?"

"Thank you, sir, but I have to leave. My mother's waiting for me for lunch."

"Any doubt of what we talked about?"

"Not at all. Thank you."

"Good. Have a nice day, then."

"Thank you very much. You, too," Alfredo says, rising.

Scanners is a complex case. The bodies are not to be shown to the relatives. The dead must stay inside the refrigerators. Families must not be informed, not even that they've been found. Nothing must be revealed to anyone about the death of the victims and their conditions. Maximum cooperation among all law enforcement agencies to separate truth and what the public opinion has to know.

Total control. Total fact containment.

Until the solution of the case. Or forever.

How many people disappear in Italy?

THE FILTHY FOUR BASTARDS: FRIDAY, 16TH OF JULY, 2:30 A.M.

Valentina can't reach her car. She can't find it. The parking lot of the Capannelle racetrack is so wide, and with no illumination.

A dreadful chirping seems to be chasing her.

In the chaos of fear, she can't remember where she left the car. An anguish with no solution. She wishes she had just asked someone to take her to dance. She only wanted to give some payback to Mario, for his carelessness, his sudden need to get a gym membership, his nights out with his friends – without her. Maybe to fool around with other women. Too proud, too jealous, she went out with the clear plan of having instant, random sex. Yes, she would have picked up anybody, to show herself that a relationship isn't a prison – for either of them. It's not genital mutilation. Valentina danced all night, but all she hooked up with was a couple glances from some idiots full of beer.

And now she's in danger, but she doesn't want to call for help. This hard rock night has gathered bikers and hippies. Radio Rock disco is a metal hammering. A deejay girl playing lots of noisy stuff. Valentina's ears ring and buzz, and she is scared to death. She has come out of the rock arena because the music's too loud. Along the lanes, toward the parking lot, something or someone growls beyond the hedges. A dog, maybe. Maybe some kind of maniac who's seen her alone and now wants to creep up on her among the cars. That hoarse breath is an adrenaline shower that makes her skin crawl. Drops of sweat roll down her arms and legs, from thighs to ankles. Anxiety has made her period burst, so she really needs a toilet. Blood is soaking her panties. She needs a tampon. But she can't go back to the arena, now – she would walk right into the stalker.

Better find the car.

The smell of blood comes to her nose, so strong. The creepy idea of a maniac aroused by her menstrual stink unleashes a carousel of fears in Valentina's heart: to be abused, beaten, killed. In a daze, she stops in the middle of the parking lot, close to a Renault 5 out of the past. She walks around the car, then she leans with her back against the driver's door. The cool metal is soothing. Valentina tries to spot her car in the dark yard, covered by silent, empty metal shells. Only one lamppost casts a weak light on the place. It's impossible to distinguish the cars from one another. She has no idea where hers can be.

But it's bound to be around, somewhere.

Terror has put Valentina inside a maze with no-fucking-body to call for help. Nobody but that presence after her, now closer yet impossibly farther. Valentina looks around, everywhere. The racetrack lights in the distance, and those from the Appian Way. She stares, slightly changing angles to hopefully detect movement, hoping to make out the shape of her car. She doesn't even turn her head; she digs into the darkness, only shifting her eyes.

Nobody. Nothing.

The horrible sound of that bestial, scraping breath seems gone.

Valentina holds her own breath to listen while the music keeps pumping from the arena. Now, she is in the middle of the deserted field of cars, covered in shadows. On the Appian Way, the traffic never stops running. She keeps holding her breath, trying to decide what to do. A tear of blood oozes out from her panties, dripping – cold and sticky – down her thigh. She doesn't care. All she can do is wait. Wait for someone who'll come to their car, and then she'll ask for help. Or even wait for everybody to leave the place – and then she'll finally spot her car in the empty lot.

How's it possible that nobody's coming?

She turns around, again and again. She leans against the Renault.

"Oh my –"

Unexpected surprise. Without words, she stares at what has silently come. Just like a bomb exploding inside her heart, a great chill runs across her body, a cold blow. Every single muscle becomes a bundle of marble, hanging dead from her brain. Total mind eclipse.

God.

Valentina has time to look at the figure at her feet. It is on all fours, and maybe it was sniffing her backside only moments before. It now stands in front of her on its paws with granitic tension. Its neck and back muscles alternate with protruding bones, drawing a pattern of primal might covered with patches of raven-black hair on cyanotic skin. The beast is the size of a Great Dane, and it seems ready to attack, as Valentina's fragile will flies away with the wind. The animal's nose sinks between her legs, under the skirt. The night doesn't throw any light on its head, its eyes. Its ears are folded back, just like black twisted horns. Its body spreads muddy flashes to the moon.

Valentina is frozen.

In her mind, her voice repeats a thousand times: *It's only a dog, it's only a huge dog.*

The Renault comes to life next to her. The driver's window slides down. A jerk looks out, speaking in a Russian accent. "Hey, sweetie. Come inside and drink vodka with us." His face is three palms away from Valentina's naked side. Fat laughs from the car.

And a cloud of alcoholic air spreads out from the rear windows, which are opening as well. The car shudders. A bunch of horny assholes. After drinking for hours inside their Renault, they didn't believe their eyes when this lovely, lonely chick got closer and closer. Astonished, they have waited in silence for the best moment to approach.

Another rotten-tooth-smiled idiot says, "We have good cocks for your cunt," before burping a laugh.

The beast suddenly springs up on its hind legs, stretching the front paws upward and screaming a grunting roar. In front of it, Valentina opens her mouth wide. She feels an abrupt languor. Right after that, she feels cold, then hot, and then cold again.

A bucketful of blood washes over the driver's face, and a second later a strange mass of flabby tubes wraps his head.

That sort of standing dog is not a dog any longer. It's something else. Its upward-stretched paws look like arms, actually, and then it lowers them on Valentina, slashing her from the face down.

Valentina watches through a lone eye, which now hangs down her face from its nerve. She discovers, with no pain at all, that those bowels coiled around the Russian driver's head are hers. The man at the wheel is trying to take them off his face while holding back his puke. The beast has gutted her. And now, all the things she didn't even know she had inside of her uncoil on the dirt below her shaking legs.

Where the fuck is pain?

The beast howls.

And in the last frame of awareness, Valentina acknowledges that at the savage call – with no hint of doubt – blood stops pouring down her legs.

The night wraps whatever happens next.

THE BATH: SATURDAY, 17TH OF JULY, 6:18 P.M.

The bathtub is ready.

It's made of iron and enameled in white. It stands on four lion's paws, and it contains about one hundred and fifty liters of hot water. It is in the middle of the empty room, shared only with a small, late-nineteenth century whitewood cabinet.

This bathroom is a cubicle isolated from all external noises. No useless furniture inside, no mirrors, only bath towels hanging from twelve-millimeter nails. A beam of daylight comes in from a vent, above the closed window.

Dark Mary comes in from the living room. She has chosen the songs "Ouroboros is Broken" and "Coda Maestoso in F" from Earth's album *Hibernaculum*, and programmed iTunes to play them in loop. She needs a long mental defragmentation in water.

DMj gets naked. She stands for a while in front of the bathtub. Her knees touch its rounded, cool edge. She has to wait some seconds as Martyna lets the music begin. The bathroom must be filled with music. Then, Mary will slowly dive, protected by such decadent melodies.

Naked in a naked room, Mary stares at the water while the music is on the air. As heavy as slow. She watches her own reflection in the water, quivering with imperceptible waves, vibrations gathered by the lion paws from the floor.

Mary's reflection is so strange.

It seems like a dream free from the laws of physics. Mary can't understand how her face really is.

What do reflections tell? Which realities do the mirrors see? And which do they let us see?

Mary enters the water.

The slow monolithic march of "Ouroboros" is a skyline of fire, a Death Valley desert sunset on motionless rocks and tumbleweed bushes rolling toward their destiny. The sun overheats voiceless living-dead. They stumble around dehydrated and mindless, looking in vain for some food, ignoring each other while they shuffle their feet slowly as continents shift. Nearsighted – though they no longer have eyes – and consumed by the starving plague, they go straight ahead, unable to change direction, bursting into an epileptic fury whenever they collide with another dead. It would seem they hate the dead. Deprived of speech, they scratch and bite, slashing and devouring one another until the weaker ends up inside the stronger, who resumes walking, keeping the same direction – as though nothing had happened – accompanied by their cloud of saprophagous flies.

The sonic odyssey of the song caresses the sweaty belly of the bathtub, which oozes drops to the floor upon its own shadow.

Mary is in the water.

Martyna can come in.

They haven't met in ten days.

A necessary pause for Martyna to defuse her crisis of jealousy. Only way to do it. She cannot dominate her inner drives; she cannot think, cannot hold steady the reins of her wild soul. Martyna lives according to the gears of obsessive compulsion and to emotional greed turned into paranoia. That seems more like a black pit in a valley of tears than a lovely shelter to be shared by two. She has to take some distance to calm her suspicion of betrayal. Anywhere, away from home, where she can dispel her delirium of extreme possessiveness. Denying herself the bed in which they sleep together. This makes the idea of Mary fucking someone else more bearable. Until Martyna, face to face with herself, finally figures out that it was only her warped mental tides. Not facts. Mary would never lie. Martyna's corrosive obsession is a gall which only poisons her own heart, instead of punishing her innocent beloved. Bulimic with love, Martyna has met and chosen Mary for her simple transparency, for her glamorous anxiety, her long black hair, because she moves softly like a black anemone, and for her dark, gothic, fetish style. She loves her subterranean personality where the old mother Yèlen still creeps – unstoppable, relentless – and blindly devours roots and worms from the humus of Mary's soul. Yèlen survives there in the depths, with guilt and sad melancholy; and giving back to her daughter all the pain of living a life between life and death, without the solace of a father.

Many times, Mary said, *Since mother's gone, I feel like living inside an empty room, with my head stuck inside the wall, floating in the crawl space and staring into the darkness between Earth and Underworld.*

How many times has Martyna been forced to realize she is unable to heal Mary's affection maladies? Such a mistake, the presumption of taking the place of Mary's mother. She believed she could make Mary forget her. Eventually, Martyna discovered she wasn't able to keep alive her early-days smile – the days when they were happy in a fairy tale burning with lust.

Whenever Martyna thinks that Mary wants to betray her – or that she's already doing that – an irrepressible rage scorches her blood. How many times did she say, *Since I've met you, my life's changed, Mary: you're my drug, my food, my happiness and sadness; without you, all I can do is keep dying.* How many? A testament to pure addiction.

Dark Mary is Martyna's full moon, able to command her repressed instincts, as well as the wounds she owes to her past, too.

Similar wounds to Mary's, but hers don't burn. They're perpetual tunnels where the putrid water of persecution flows. Martyna's mother, Tamsen, was an alcoholic, a nihilist, oppressive and incestuous. Haughty and obscene, she keeps digging wormholes, cowardly hiding under Martyna's soul and psychic floor. She kept on surviving, never stopping to speak her contempt about her daughter; Tamsen, a mother who spent her life trying to make her daughter drink, too, so as to abuse her.

You ain't shit, Martyna. Can't you see? Look here, where you came out from. Come on, kiss my cunt or I'll beat you. You smell like it, you fucking bitch.

Mary is fragile, a bit neurotic, but she doesn't try to off herself with chemicals; she only moves sonic storms, maybe to annihilate the underground-digging Yèlen, always nibbling at the stockpiles of Mary's souls.

On the other hand, Martyna desperately loves her mother, Tamsen; that's a fact, and she misses her to death. But she acts the other way round. She has elected Mary as Tamsen's substitute, and that resulted in summoning pain, and more pain for both of them, endlessly, never to find satisfaction, never to find the nectar of her own existence.

It's a real battle, victim against executioner. Dark Mary can hardly dam Martyna's intemperance, trying to keep an emotional and physical distance, saving herself a bunch of hours thanks to her nomadic job. Leaving Martyna to chew on her furious insecurities until her jealousy drops below the horizon. Sometimes, when Martyna's sense of possession reaches the boiling point, Mary deliberately strews the suspect of betrayal to neutralize her Othello. That always works like a homeopathic treatment. But only temporarily. Martyna can only try to calm down staying away from Mary, thinking her beloved deejay could be missing her. That she could be needing her, desiring her.

Back from the party at Goa's, Dark Mary found an empty house. She stood there, waiting for Martyna, lost in a limbo of doubts, relief, and other flying thoughts of sparkling loss.

"Martyna, where have you been?"

"Gone out, driving around," she says, with a soft sigh. "I needed to escape from these walls for a bit." Her quiet words are oil trickling onto the water, over the dripping sounds of the bathtub.

It's very hot outside, and Mary is so tired; very weak and tired. "Were you upset with me because I didn't bring you with me to Asia's party?" Mary asks as Martyna softly wipes her shoulder and breasts with a sponge.

"I was hurt. But in the end, I thought that it's all right. It's all right, honey. Now you're here and it's all right."

"I didn't like coming back home and finding nobody."

"So, would you have been happier if you came back and found someone else?" Martyna asks, hardly holding back her jealousy. "Come on, honey. Just kidding."

Dark Mary doesn't laugh, doesn't smile. She lets the woman scrub her skin, while hot water polishes the rest of her body with salt, bay leaves, and melted clay.

"Well, tell me. How was this birthday party? Did you meet Asia Argento?"

"They had a private table on the balcony, and her friends made a human chain all around. No way."

"I guess looky-loos complicated matters."

"Security let through only people on the list."

"But you were."

"Too many people between me and Asia. I couldn't even see her."

"Why didn't you call her?"

"Couldn't. The music was too loud."

"Oh, sure. Your deejay friend playing."

"Yeah, I saw him."

"Did you talk to him?"

"I didn't want to. But I got some new ideas to round out my set."

"Something he played?"

"Oh, no. He plays too much Italian stuff. You know those melodies hurt me. Rock is a language between player and listener. Rock lyrics must not be understood; they are an instrument; they have to be listened to. That's why, in Italy, Anglo-American rock culture is timeless, while Italian popular music is a byproduct of opera. When I play around Europe, maybe I can set a few Italian songs. A couple, maybe. Bluvertigo, Subsonica. Nothing more. I can't set together Sex Pistols and operetta. Italian records lack that specific beat and sound." Music aside, Mary hit a nerve.

"Are you still thinking of leaving?"

"Martyna, we have to deal with reality."

"Please, never forget that this is your home." The possibility of Mary leaving, sooner or later, holds Martyna in never-ending alert.

"Exactly. I can come back whenever I want. But I need to travel, as you know. I can't stay in a cage. Overall, I have to try and loosen my relationship with my mother."

"Yèlen is dead. Just like my mother. We only have to accept the —"

Mary cuts her off in a sharp tone. "I need to change the subject."

"I love staying here. In this house," Martyna reveals after a long, wise pause. "I can stay here, when you leave, so I —"

"When I'll be here, you'll be, too. Would you wash my hair, now, please?" Mary says, interrupting her again.

"Yes." Today, Martyna is more forgiving than ever.

Out of the Goa, that night, Mary was noticed by two young strangers, rather drunk and cheery from coke-snorting.

Their vacation's just started, and they're hungry for females. They're blond-haired bodybuilders, and could impress and fuck a lot of loser girls in Rome. Some double penetration would be ideal.

They chase Mary down Libetta Street. They speak almost perfect Italian, but Mary flipping them off isn't good at all – for her own good. They laugh, then let her reach her car. Then they go on to their rental vehicle.

Mary turns the engine on and hits the gas pedal. She pretends not to notice them, and drives slowly. She wants those guys to follow her. The two of them laugh, and do just that. Now, Mary waves with a hand out the window, so the deed is done. The two blonds flash their headlights and laugh once again. They've walked right into it.

Dark Mary takes a look at her fingernails, decorated with a special, steel French manicure – lacquered in shiny red and little white daises. An idea from a friend, street-art painter and blacksmith. She picks up her Hello Kitty purse and throws it on the backseat. As she does that, she involuntary slashes the passenger seat open with her nails.

The padding comes out from three deep gashes.

Martyna dampens Mary's hair, then rubs her head with a generous dose of ginger Body Shop shampoo, in circular, slow movements.

"You said you got some new ideas for your set."

"I want to explore the EBM. I could play some of the heavier electro-hard. I mean, Trent Reznor, Tool, Ministry. But American hardcore punk, too. I don't know. Maybe."

"A lot of avant-garde noise."

"I can't certainly play 70s rock and roll," Mary says. She knows she entered one of her partner's musical dead ends. "Punk rock's okay. Hard rock's okay. Rock and roll, no."

"I just keep saying that Kiss's 'I Was Made for Loving You' could make a lot of people happy." Martyna pauses. "*Betrayed* aside."

"I have to work with big sound, raging melodies and medium time. 'I Was Made' couldn't make anybody happy. Strictly speaking, it would dig a hole in the global sound and excitement of the whole set. I can't risk freezing my gig."

"Well. You know how it works. It's your job."

"Sure. It's my job."

Martyna isn't music-smart. And she doesn't want to piss off Mary; she must not speak about her job. Better to ignore her. A bit of peace, for once. "Do you like it if I massage you like this?"

"I ... I feel nothing."

Dark Mary recalls her gig at the Capannelle racetrack. Fifteen thousand people dancing under the stage. An earthquake. A DJ set of only half an hour, but the whole Radio Rock crew was there for her, to be centrifuged by queen Dark Mary. A mob scene, a real ocean made of heads and arms, human waves pushed and pulled by Mary's short track list. A dozen bomb-songs in medium time, starting with Greenday's "American Idiot."

However, in spite of the army of fans come for her, Dark Mary didn't feel any pleasure, nor the glorious impact with the crowd. She didn't felt the sadistic chill of rising over that mass of people and taking control of thirty thousand legs, managing their heartbeats, focus and sweat, tasting the admiration of that militia. She signed autographs for an hour, did sketches, impressed kisses on diaries and paper towels. She posed for a lot of pictures. At last, she gave someone one of her own *Night of the Living Dead* T-shirts as a gift, the one she used during the set. She didn't feel any emotion during the whole, great gig.

Just like she felt nothing on the crime scene in the parking lot, around that Renault car.

Supine, disarranged on the ground, near the Renault, there was a girl; a beautiful girl, though her face had been marred by claws and teeth. Should that girl have been alive and *intact*, Mary would have probably tried to seduce her. But she laid there on the dirt, her head tilted on her shoulder, chin abnormally trapped in the notch of her collarbone. Her hair clotted in a throng of grit and blood. Her bowels protruding from a huge cut from throat to pubis, crowning the whole body in a garden of flakes of fat tissue, torn flesh, tendons, and nerves uncoiled with senseless violence. Her blood-covered legs twisted at right angles, almost tracing a half-swastika. Her shoes still on.

Mary stared inside the car, at the dead driver still sitting at the wheel. The man's eyes were out of his head, his cheeks and tongue mauled. His head hung out the window, neck broken, ear to the door and mouth wide. Behind his upside-down head, his left arm was eaten to the bone. There were two passengers, lying cuddled as two little brothers, their heads sunk against each other's shoulder. They sat on a happy storm of slashed guts and muscles torn and wrecked with merciless lacerations and randomly inflicted bites. One of them had his face unfurled from his nape to his chin. The inside of the mask was now a bloody bib on the victim's chest. His scalp joined the feast of bowels pulled out from his belly. Guts, blood, and excrement turned the backseat into a rotten swamp around his hips, thighs, calves, and feet; it all leaked down on the car floor, over empty bottles of beer and vodka, an old copy of *Pravda*, cans, plastic cups, X-rated magazines, and Russian street-market junk. By some miracle, his friend's features were intact, but his wide-open eyes – immortalized in death – still seized the terror, the fear, the absurd. After watching them, Mary walked around the car. The passenger seat was vacant.

A fourth man had been aboard. He left his smell on the seat. Tiny drops of blood ran from there toward Appian Way, toward daylight. Slightly sad for that loss, Dark Mary had to leave the scene of the massacre: the racetrack was about to close, and the crowd was coming out and approaching the parking lot. With her boots, she scrambled the footmarks on the dirt, then ran to her Volkswagen before anybody could see her and rally her fans again.

"Give me your hands, Mary," Martyna says.

"Thank you. I guess they're dirty." Mary lays her palms on the edge of the tub, dropping out from the memory of that strange night. Feeling a certain remorse for the fourth man, who escaped the Renault slaughter, Mary decides to give in to Martyna's attentions. Something unresolved lingers in the air, and inside Mary's mind. She has to keep it out. Figure out how to leave Rome. Get away, fast. Say nothing to anyone, and let Martyna take care of her.

Martyna loves giving Mary a bath. It's the only contact Mary grants her without fearing Martyna's voracious fever. Martyna can caress her, touch her, brush her – a practice in which Mary loves to abandon herself. She doesn't like the greed for sex. She prefers that evolved grooming. It's more useful. Instead of what Martyna yearns, Dark Mary needs gentleness. It's a steadfast cohesion of egotisms, opposing forces, like two magnets of the same polarity. Martyna steps around the tub and takes Mary's right hand. A scar on the back, a little pale loop Martyna finds sexy, and that she'd have to shoot with a macro lens.

During three years of a fickle relationship, Martyna has taken more than twenty-four thousand pictures. She needs an infinite gallery of details to sew together in a big portrait poster. She wants to compose Mary's face using all the photos, to make a sort of Nativity on a quasi-Bruegel background of skeletons and bodies, to describe a love sacred and bloodily divine. It will have to be her very first composition, the testament to her love for Dark Mary above all, above her own creative world. Maybe that little scar could be the starting stigmata, the baseline for the whole conception. All in trichrome: red, yellow, blue, and refined with white glow to focus Mary's spiritual purity.

Non-God's mother. Rock necro-Madonna.

Dark brown lines of old blood fill the gaps under Mary's nails.

Martyna stares at Mary's eyes.

Martyna stares at Mary's eyes.

Mary stares at Martyna's eyes.

SOME HOURS BEFORE, ELSEWHERE

The Baume & Mercier watch at Alfredo's wrist marks 7:30 a.m., sharp.

Daylight slants.

So, that fucked-up Renault 5 is parked on the dirt lot of the racetrack as though it were a crashed spaceship. No life inside, but an incredible story written upon the wake of its own destiny.

The Police have cordoned off and surrounded the zone, forbidding access to and from all directions of Capannelle Street, and have covered the crime scene with a huge tensile structure to block the wind before it can blow grit over traces, or carry away anything useful – hair, skin flakes, blood, and saliva kneaded with dirt – in a thirty-meter radius.

The passenger's door is open.

Footprints of struggle in the dirt.

Someone has escaped the killer.

Marshal Alfredo is not a dupe, and he can read what the dirt tells on the crime scene – a story someone has tried to erase at night. The murderer is not so smart; that's a fact. He's not a real serial killer at all. He doesn't plan, and he doesn't even act following some psychotic script. He seems to kill according to an almost innocent impulse. Better: pure. One should say *not human.* And, more exactly, *animal.*

The motive of these brutal killings is the hyena, probably – or bear – at his leash; namely, its feeding. It would sound more sensible to give the beast the human meat it needs inside its cage, but its master isn't driven to chase and take out people. He isn't able to do such things; he possesses neither the will nor the physical prowess.

So, why not just buy meat at the butcher's?

Because the master cannot afford thirty pounds of meat a day.

Why doesn't he just get rid of the beast? Why doesn't he surrender it to the State Forestry, or to a zoo? Why doesn't he kill it?

Maybe because its chromosomes have the ability to change, as they did even in the test tube. That animal is some kind of rare specimen, maybe unique, maybe some lab freak that must be protected and kept hidden. This can be listed as a *Scanners* case. These four victims haven't had their skulls drilled, but their bodies were slaughtered by the anthropophagic beast.

"So, that's seven," the Marshal mutters to Fildor under his mustache.

"Nine, if we count those two on the Casilina," Fildor replies, with his Parker silver pen against his lips.

"Do you think they're related?"

"All the men here are from Russia. The girl is local. The two on the Casilina weren't Italian, either. A group of strangers. Maybe they could be friends?"

"I'd say no," Vanacura says. "I've got no idea, actually. Or maybe I have too many fanciful thoughts about this. Those two were drained of all their blood, then someone ripped out their hearts in a pretty methodical way. That would be a first for him."

"First we've found. That's different," Fildor says, correcting.

"Sure."

"Here, we have a savage animal," Fildor says. "And someone else trafficking in blood and organs at the same time." He seems distracted by the mute car of the dead. "Perhaps he's the same person, unleashing his beast against whomever he doesn't deem fit to become a 'donor,'" he says, making the "quotation marks" sign to rile the Marshal. Alfredo hates that gesture.

"Too complicated. Doesn't add up. Inside this fucking car, last night, three people died. These two crimes have nothing in common," Alfredo says. "And we missed one. Maybe still alive."

"True. And these have only been mauled, not drilled. I'll bring these new friends in for autopsy as soon as possible."

"Should I pass by tonight at eight?" Alfredo asks.

"Don't even try it, mate. I'm too old for that," Fildor whispers as the bodies are loaded on the Mortuary truck. "I can have these four done for *tomorrow* at eight."

"Okay, I tried. See you tomorrow," Alfredo says, glancing at his watch. He then puts on his legendary white hat.

"I'll be waiting at my lab. We can have pizza," Fildor says.

"Oh, no, you know I hate eating among corpses. We can go to the *marble tables* in Trastevere."

"Such subtle humor," Fildor says, sneering.

Meeting at the pizzeria nicknamed *Obituary*.

JUST LIKE THE HOLY SHROUD. A NEARBY HOUSE IN ROME, 4:25 P.M., PIGNETO DISTRICT

The *Night of the Living Dead* T-shirt hangs on the wall in a frame. Perfectly stretched and protected by glass. No hands can touch or wash it.

Claudia's room.

Dark Mary's T-shirt is on the wall among rock posters, display cases, postcards, and pictures. A brand new idol.

Claudia has called in her friends: Marcella, Benedetta, and Mirco, all Dark Mary fans. They are sort of a DMj church.

They sit on the floor, watching the evidence in religious gathering and with fervent agony. Four young emo-core guys, veterans of the unforgettable night at the racetrack.

Marcella has posted on Facebook words that tell everything about their elation: *We have touched Her, She touched us and then a river of black tears poured out, inside our hearts, destroying every light.* Statement enriched by a heart emoticon, three +s, and an extra heart.

"I can't believe it. It's really the shirt She wore last night."

"She gave it to me when She came out to greet the first rows. I was there."

"Are you sure it's Hers?"

"Yes, I do. She – in person – gave it to me. She held it under her arm. She wanted to give it to us. I was lucky. I stared at Her eyes. She looked at my eyes."

"What a pity I wasn't near you, Claudia. Too much crowd. She had it on when she played. After the show, She put on a Cure shirt."

The living dead printed on the T-shirt looked down on the four of them.

"But I must say a very weird thing to you," Claudia says.

"What?"

"When I took that shirt in my hand ..."

"So what?"

"C'mon, talk!"

"Claudia, please!"

"First, give me a beer, please," Claudia says.

Mirco hands her a bottle.

"What happened, Claudia?"

"Let her drink," Mirco says. "Don't you see she's crying?"

"I'm so sorry," Claudia says with a gulp. The beer is too cold for her tears. "Well, when She gave me Her shirt ... I mean ... when I *touched* that shirt ... how can I say it ... it wasn't soaked with sweat."

"What the hell are you saying? She must have taken it off right after the show, and it got dry."

"Bullshit. She wore that shirt for the whole set. Then, she immediately came off the stage to meet us. Five minutes. It couldn't have dried already."

"Okay, so the T-shirt wasn't soaked. So what?"

"What's the problem with you?" Claudia asks, protesting. "I'm telling you the shirt wasn't *wet* at all."

"Maybe She took Hers. That's just a double, to use as a gift."

"I don't think so," Claudia replies before taking another sip. "That shirt still has Her smell."

"Maybe she sprayed Her perfume on it."

"No, guys."

"Claudia, what the fuck are you saying?"

PART TWO
TRASHING

San Luigi dei Francesi church, Santa Giovanna d'Arco Street.
Half past eight a.m. Mass is beginning.
Far from sun and heat, Father Sebastiano waits for some relief, standing in the cool shadows of the vestry. The chronic disease that has been afflicting him for many years has by now somehow normalized. This means he can maintain a degree of control over it, to face the power of daylight without major risks for his photophobia and hypersensitivity to the sun. All he has to do is constantly move from one shadow zone to the next. In the church, there is a young priest who can stand in for him when Sebastiano is sick. The Holy See has given Sebastiano a simple task, which allows him to stay in Rome, permanent posting, to exploit his great talent as scholar researching History of Religions.

At 8:28, Sebastiano was forced to leave his flock just before the beginning of Mass. A violent coughing fit caused him to hand over the rite to Don Severino. He ran away to the bathroom of the church.

The opening hymn is sung over the horrible sounds of the pale priest, who's spitting his daily instalment out: that damn black clay coming up from his lungs. He ate a new soul, last night, at the Bambin Gesù hospital: from Carmelo, a terminal kid. The porphyria-sick priest was ready to welcome the faithful and sing the hymn, but he felt a sudden, acidic, warm geyser climbing his trachea to reach the uvula. He almost regurgitated a black gush on his cassock in front of those people. He ran down the altar, reached the vestry and then the bathroom to throw up the dark cream into the sink.

The matter had filled his mouth entirely.

8:33. Father Sebastiano takes a look in the mirror after having cried and hacked in the sink. He sees his eyes blushed and swollen. He sees his face white like chalk, teeth and lips dark brown. To feed on souls involves feeding on death. There's no cure, no remedy until God chooses, until He decides to stop this. While Mass continues, Sebastiano gathers his sputum in a glass jar. Then, he puts it inside a closed shelf on the bookcase, waiting for sunset to bring it home. He will have to talk Don Severino into letting him go home alone. Severino owns a car, and usually drives Sebastiano home at night. But tonight, Sebastiano already has company in a glass jar. As his breath calms, Sebastiano descends underground, where he keeps something that must never be out in the open, out of God's house, something nobody must see. Sebastiano has an hour, while Severino says Mass.

How old are the subterranean conduits branching off under the church? Nobody knows. Even Sebastiano doesn't know who dug them, and when. All Sebastiano needs is those dark nooks to orient himself from one corridor to the next. The nooks contain many amazing treasures: golden items, relics. But none of that is really important. Sebastiano is the only one who knows every meter of that underworld; anyone would get lost in a bunch of steps, and would die down there together with any secret they discovered. Sebastiano has created the most important secret.

He must go down three staircases in the dark. The gloom and heavy air in the shafts under the church are the perfect atmosphere for his disease. The high humidity manages to keep compressed the black mass inside Sebastiano's lungs. But the priest knows that's a temporary truce. His pupils dilate completely, optic nerves almost giving a sense of pleasure as the priest goes down into the deep, sweet absence of light. The pale priest prefers to keep the light bulbs turned off to make his way into the burrows. He delays the time of pain as much as he can; until he reaches the nook he's looking for, he can go on blindly. He follows his nose. As he did many times before, he feels that trail of flesh-smell through the air.

Eighteenth nook in the bricks, among bulwarks of clay maybe

under the Tiber's riverbed, or the foundations of the Corte di Cassazione. The last nook of that dark labyrinth; and it can be lit, now, after fifteen minutes of quick walking. Father Sebastiano turns on the small light over his hidden treasure.

There is an old bed base leaning on the wall. Hanged to the mesh from iron hooks are a dozen human hearts. Twelve cardiac muscles still pulsating. They are drenched, warm, anonymous, and trickle little drops of what blood they have left of their past lives. There is no soul Sebastiano could eat inside any of those hearts. He cannot suck the spiritual sap from those human pieces for himself, because they don't have the slightest intention of stopping and dying. And if the pale priest tries to drink something from the cut blood vessels, a weird and bitter taste fills his mouth. Like listening to the sound of sea in a seashell. As Sebastiano breathes in the air from the empty muscles, in his mind he sees all the life-scenes for which those atria and ventricles have beaten. No souls inside them, but the old owner's memories as filmic storage, a stormy and colored sixty-second lighting flash of existence, always ending the same way: chest opened by a stranger's hand – always the same hand – and the heart ripped out of the body. It's a phantasmagorical and ectoplasmic tale that ends and starts again in a loop. No variations at all. A sort of physiological movie.

Father Sebastiano has read the cardiac contents of all the twelve still-beating hearts he protects within the true peace of God. He must examine all of them, every time a new one arrives.

A new heart brings new doubts with itself, a wider horizon of lights and chances.

The heart with the least impurities shall be the chosen one.

The hearts are delivered to Sebastiano by one person. That person has a project, an absolute need.

"But you know," Sebastiano whispers, thinking aloud in a soft voice as he addresses that person in his mind, "that is crazy. There is no guarantee. God will painfully punish us for what we are doing."

Ex-Marshal Vanacura is in a private residence on Tiziano Street, Parioli district near the Bioparco. It's 8:45 a.m. at his Baume & Mercier watch. A mailman got suspicious because of the disgusting stench coming from the garden of the old widow, Mrs. Ricci, who didn't answer her entry phone. He called the Carabinieri. Agents broke into the house to find, in the backyard, the corpse of a young man in advanced decomp.

Fildor is in the morgue, at work, but Alfredo doesn't need a degree to recognize the latest of his *Scanners*. The special Carabinieri squad has to use an ultrasonic shotgun to kick out the swarm of flies entirely covering the body. The victim seems to have died many days ago. All over the rotten bluish flesh, the confused statement of its abusers can be read. Like the other, the boy's head has exploded, his face intact under brow ridge and ears and the first cervical vertebrae.

The rest of the body shows the usual array of swollen hems, gashes dilated by greasy suppuration, foams of liquefied tissues where ants are marching, absurd sores where they could stick three fingers and also a smartphone. Divots of brain join the white gravel depicting the unmistakable head-burst pattern, happened close to a fountain where the old lady apparently plugged the hose to water her garden.

The Marshal remembers the San Camillo hospital body. That victim had sought water, too, before dying.

"Where's the lady?" Alfredo asks through a handkerchief held to his mouth. The fumes of putrefaction burn in his eyes.

"She's an in-patient at Regina Margherita clinic," Corporal Lofusco replies.

"Thank you," Alfredo says. "I need breakfast."

Dark Mary is vegetating.

Since last Saturday night.

Lying on the bed. On her back, motionless.

Martyna is around taking pictures, out of Rome. Looking for a scoop. Her friend Damaso, a young journalist, has driven her to the chapel of rest at a funeral home managed by a friend of his. There are two young sisters who had died in a brutal car crash along Salaria Road. The bodies have been cleaned and put back together, with huge seams along almost-wax skin. Paying one hundred euros to the manager, Martyna can take pictures of the naked bodies. Damaso's friend is a bona fide undertaker, as well as a sort of dealer of the dead, since a corpse is a commodity for him. He has a great sense of humor and he hates all the music of the world except the one song, Kraftwerk's "We Are the Robots." A body is like a car; a cemetery is like a junkyard.

Martyna left Rome suddenly, Saturday around 8:15 p.m.. Mary didn't know anything about it. So, she immediately decided to cancel that night's DJ set at Radio Rock Beach, as well as Sunday's night show at the Alcatraz, near Fiumicino Airport. Lately, Martyna has begun to go out, often by herself. Despite her will to stay with her Mary forever, she is trying to stay away as much as possible. The couple needs some breathing space. She lies and lies about working engagements – except for the two-sister scoop, about which she could furnish proof, though nobody could be less interested – and that makes her an even more sordid coward. Her behavior is mortifying, as well as her abuse with Monster, Red Bull, absinthe, whisky and her bohemian decadence with her new radical chic friends – morons addicted to the next guy's cigarettes, and with a shiny iPhone always in their back pocket.

Mary wants to stay alone.

Without music.

Without words.

Without people.

Without thoughts.

Without bullshit.

Dark Mary discovers her own smooth skin in the dark.

There's a small bar close to the butcher's.

It's 9:27 in the morning, Bologna square. Uncanny desolation all around.

While Alfredo Vanacura has breakfast, he feels like the most stupid guy in the world. Urban waste seems to fill his soul with responsibility, especially for all those murdered kids. As days go by, people's heads keep exploding, while other guys get robbed of their heart and blood. The world is looping the loop in a fucking funfair.

Something's going more than wrong.

And life, this damn life, for men who are really alone, has become a cow carcass that rots in the living room watching a talent show on TV.

Life goes mad; goes without saying.

Is it the climate change? Is it some sort of mass miscarriage? Is humanity the world's hernia? Why do we work so hard if everything must fall into ruins? Isn't it foolish to torment our souls?

A well-tanned man – about sixty, potbellied, dressed in ivory white linen suit, unbuttoned red shirt, straw hat, white loafers, and black mustache and goatee like an anchovy on sweaty chin, cigar between fingers – exits the butcher shop with a slice of pizza. He bites into it with moaning pleasure. But it's not pizza. It's raw meat. Pink, shiny, and thick-cut.

Traffic noise like distant undertow.

Across the dark sides of the empty walls, the neighbors' muffled steps flow. They're unknown; they're alone, too, and therefore speechless.

The day is rising, but Dark Mary will wait for dusk. She floats motionless on the bed, thinking of life passing by without her.

Level 3, room 34.

"Marshal, I rely on your good sense," doctor Zwoul says. He has blue eyes and milky-white hair. "Mrs. Ricci's heart is as fragile as a canary. One more strong emotion and she's a goner."

"I got it, doctor. Thank you," Alfredo whispers before entering the room.

Giuliana Ricci, born 1928. Since 2002, she's the widow of Wolfgang, former Air Force official. Retiree, with no sons. Landowner, no heirs, alone in her herbicidal, sneaky stinginess. No maid, no cook, no company at all. Housework is what keeps her alive. She does landscaping and crosswords to train both pencil and mind, and follows a rich diet of essays and novels. Once a week, she instructs the Indian Ramir to go shopping for her, taking advantage of his legendary good-neighbor altruism. Until one night she sees a boy entering her garden. He climbs the fence and stops among the potted flowers in front of her door. Then, he walks around the house. The sun is down. The lady looks out the window, keeping the living room lights off. She puts on her glasses and notices the stranger is lethally wounded and covered in blood. She takes the cordless phone to call the police. The boy has reached the fountain, then he tries to turn on the faucet, but he falls on the ground, hands to his head. It looks like a terrible pain is burning his brain.

"So, what else did you see, Madam?" Alfredo asks.

"I don't want to recount what I saw, Marshal. I'll never do it. I'm sorry," Giuliana says in a soft voice. "I was about to call the police but I hung up as I watched that poor boy have a sort of epileptic fit. Seconds later, I felt sick myself, and I called Ramir. Just as he picked up, I had a heart attack. Thank God I woke up in here."

After meeting the old lady, the Marshal reaches the bus stop in Bologna square. Two obese women are waiting for the same line, 62, back to Torre Argentina. Alfredo's home office in the old Jewish ghetto.

Giuliana, that stingy old woman, saw the unknown boy crashing to the ground and squirming until his head opened up like popcorn. This confirms that the victims don't die after the beast assaults them, not until their heads explode.

It is apparent there's nothing logical about the nature of these extraordinary facts.

However, intuition scratches inside Alfredo's brain:

Why doesn't anybody see the beast? How is it possible that the victims survive those deadly maulings? Why do the beast's isolated chromosomes spontaneously change? What the hell is Fildor doing at the morgue, now, instead of coming to Ricci's house? What if one of the victims wakes up on the autopsy table while Fildor is cutting them?

And, over all, *why the fuck isn't the 62 here yet?*

The temperature of the day is rising; heat burns.
Walls are warming.
Dark Mary closes her eyes, enjoying her muscles and tendons

relax. Not a single joint is working, now. She must not stand, nor dance. She's letting herself go, completely.

If Martyna were out of her life forever, everything would be different, and wonderfully light.

Do I really need her? How can she create such a negative disturbance for her own life?

Had she the courage, she'd kill her.

She could pay someone to do that.

Better to avoid such thoughts. Better to give the brain some peace.

Dark Mary drives her mind toward a brook shore, colorless water running under her eyes over the smooth stones of its bed. Among mulberries and magnolias, stripes of light across tree crowns.

Using a fingertip, she writes words on the water – small haikus the flowing water takes away from her. Maybe, at the mouth of the river, between rocks, all the writings cluster in a book of liquid pages, thin veils of transparent words.

It's a quarter past eight in the afternoon. Father Sebastiano is leaving the church. He holds a paper bag hiding the glass jar with his sputum inside. His lungs can breathe fresh air, so they give a short, but powerful cough. Oxygen is not a friend of his inner guest. But this is not a good time, not here, on the street. Sebastiano must expel his black magma at home, where he feels safe. He never throws away what the souls leave inside him. And he doesn't even know what could happen to that clay in daylight. Every ounce of it must be kept in the dark, like the hearts locked underground. The soul drain that Sebastiano feeds on is fine black dirt, ultra-thick odorless petroleum that sparkles like graphite. His respiratory system is a cave wherein human souls deposit their scum. In part, they are expectorated; in part, they stagnate at the bottom of his alveoli, a permanent crust that hardly flakes under his most violent hacking. No expert had the opportunity of studying that wretched dirt. No doctor can try to heal him. This is Sebastiano's secret, bonded to other secrets nobody must know, that nobody would understand. Things belonging to this and the other world. God is the only one who can manage Sebastiano's mystery, letting Mother Nature do her course all the way, as it is written in the plot of existence.

Father Sebastiano is home, now, an old flat near the Pantheon, 44 Orfani Street.

Lighting is very dim, so the pale priest can feel sheltered. The stale air, as well, allows him to maintain control over his coughing fits.

Inside the dark guest room, the woman on the chair has given birth to a new casting of red flesh, now on the floor. Thank God that all the windows are hermetically closed; otherwise, a storm of flies would have invaded the house by now. Sebastiano must also manage his flatmate's matter, too, motionless manufacturer of living meat: warmish, fibrous, smelly, rich with collagen and tender at the touch. The organic cream dissolves in water like sugar, and then gets lost through the gorgeous stomach of Rome's sewer system.

"Good evening, Susanna," Sebastiano says to his silent flatmate. "How are you?"

She doesn't answer.

Moving through darkness, Sebastiano reaches the small round table where he can put his glass jar of black clay. He opens the lid, picks up some of the hot matter with his fingers. He rubs some of it on Susanna's naked shoulder, which absorbs it instantly.

"Here we go. Now let's clean up what's on the floor. You soiled your feet, Susanna."

The latest mudslide of flesh covers the floor from Susanna's feet to the door. And every time he removes the meaty slime from the tiles, Sebastiano seems to hear it softly murmuring. Dozens of voices: men, women, and children too. Incomprehensible conversations dying out as the pale priest throws the matter in the toilet and flushes.

It's twenty past eight at night.

The *Obituary*, in Trastevere, is overcrowded as usual, even on a Monday.

Peroni beer, good food, pizza and pasta and lightly fried food, quickly served. You can sit inside, or at the sidewalk tables under white sunshades and with high bushes sheltering you from the crazy traffic and street smog only two steps away. Inside, the *Obituary* has two rooms, one larger with a view of the firewood oven and pizza-makers at work; the other, a hall ending with the toilets. All the tables are wooden frames with slabs of grey marble. No tablecloths; the customers eat directly on the cold travertine. That's how this pizza restaurant got its nicknames: *Marble Tables*, and *Obituary*.

Alfredo and Fildor sit along the street boundary, getting poisoned at every honking vehicle driving by. As they wait for *supplì*, stuffed zucchini flowers, and *olive ascolane*, Alfredo keeps checking his wristwatch, Fildor busy with his smartphone. The dead-cutter, strangely quiet, seems to have turned into a telex. Ex Marshal Alfredo is discreetly peeking at a couple of women, about forty, eating at a nearby table; they often glance at him, whisper, and smile. Finally, the appetizers arrive.

"Well. Let's eat," Vanacura says in a resigned tone. His heart has palpitations at the very thought of standing and stepping toward the ladies, playing gallant and saying, *Hello, let me introduce us: my friend, there, cuts corpses; me, I seek people whose heads explode after death. Would you have a beer with us?*

"Oh, yes. Sorry, man," Max Fildor replies, putting his phone back in his pocket.

"Are you all right? You look nervous."

"I've been working like crazy since Saturday, that's all. I think I slept seven hours out of forty-eight." Then, Fildor brings to his mouth a too-hot fried olive. "Holy fuck."

"There. Drink up, mate," Alfredo says, pouring some cold beer into his glass.

"Thank you, Alfredo. This case ... this case is fucking madness. My lab is a mess of bodies. Just as you start cutting one, then ..."

"Then ... what?"

"Another comes. It seems like working at a post office counter. It's insane," Fildor says, shaking his head and looking down. "It's insane." He looks like he's about to cry.

"Are you tired? Can't you ask someone to stand in?"

"What? Oh, no," Fildor says, as though someone were giving an electroshock to his butt. "No way. I must go on."

"Don't panic. Consider this an opportunity." The ex-Marshal swallows an olive after cooling it in the beer. Normally, he'd never do something that gross – what's worse, with the two ladies noticing. But right now Alfredo is peering into Fildor's brain. It needs vivisection. Something's not right. Fildor is strangely troubled, more than ever. The most unflappable pathologist in Italy is having a breakdown. He cut up thirty years' worth of bodies. Tonight, though, his legendary fortitude is elsewhere, or gone altogether. Such unusual news. The man in front of Vanacura is now white pulp with no shell. He can smell its fresh smell.

"Not to mention other bodies, for our case, that are about to come," Alfredo says. His voice is like a thunder to his mate's ears. Fildor almost chokes on an olive. He coughs hard. "Not a good day for olives," Vanacura suggests. "I asked for two dozen patrols to comb through every cranny of the city," he explains. "Riverbanks, under the bridges on Tiber and Aniene, deserted silos, train yards, overpasses, canals, and gutters between East Rome and North Rome, and everywhere else with water and wild, overgrown areas. It should be easy; the killer seems not to have the time to bury or take away the bodies. Either the time, or the strength."

"Did the Prefect really give you all these men?"

"He had to. We've already found four dry maggots, that –"

"What did you find?" Fildor asks, eyes open wide.

"Please, don't stop me all the time. Dry maggots, dead early this year, maybe last autumn, and –"

"Jesus Christ, Alfredo, what the hell do you mean ... '*dry maggots*?'"

"Let me finish .... Dry maggots are bodies without blood and heart."

A man with long hair, sitting at the table beside Alfredo, stops their exchange. "Sirs, if I'm going to vomit, I'll make sure to turn your way."

The Marshal apologizes with a cough.

Fildor whispers, "What do these maggots have in common with the head-bursters?"

"They must be related. Something tells me they are."

Fildor's eyes lower on his dish, where he's killing a stuffed zucchini flower with his fork.

Pizzas come. "*Capricciosa* for the Marshal," the waiter announces. "*Margherita* with mushrooms for the dead-cutter," he says to Fildor.

The pathologist stares at the mushroom party on the hot, melted mozzarella.

"C'mon, Fildor. Eat it. You need to."

"Oh, I can't. I feel sick. Sorry, I think I'm going home."

"Why?"

"I told you. I don't feel like it. I just want to go."

"No way. Eat this fucking pizza and then we go home together."

"I said no. Please, don't push, Alfredo. Waiter …" he calls.

"All right. Me, I'm eating up." The Marshal gives up. He's hungry, after all. Nervously chewing, he feels a growing bitterness he can't understand, and this makes him feel like a jerk.

The waiter comes along. Fildor asks for the bill. He pulls out from his pocket his silver pen and credit card. His hands tremble, so the pen flies away, bouncing on the ground. The pathologist stands up to recover it. "Fuck, my Parker," he growls through his teeth. He steps toward it and reaches down, but involuntary kicks the pen, making it skid farther and onto an iron grating. Fatally, the pen drops underground. Fildor straightens with a dopey look on his face – the portrait of childish astonishment. Something's happening inside his mind. The Marshal is worried about it. He rises from the marble table, leaving a quarter of pizza untouched, and passes by the two women he was stealing glances with before. This time, they don't watch him. Maybe those two fellows looked a little too much like an old, nervous gay couple.

Alfredo flanks Fildor, who stares at nothing through the iron grating. His favorite pen is lost in the dark.

"Hey, mate. Are you all right? You look like your ghost just died."

Fildor doesn't seem to get Alfredo's wit. But he comes to his senses as his friend touches his shoulder.

"I have to get home. Sorry," Fildor says.

"That's okay. I'll take you home."

"Alfredo, you can't," Fildor softly whispers.

"Why not?"

"Because you don't have a car."

Motionless since two days ago, lying on the bed, Dark Mary could remain forever in this state. But she's starting to feel thirsty, and hungry.

David doesn't look well. But he's an animal; he'll be okay. He has everything he needs inside his terrarium.

Time. She doesn't care about time. The only kind of time she knows, the only thing worth thinking about, is the beat of her songs. Martyna is still out, and she'll be back home when Mary will be playing, tonight – all night long. David and music are all she loves. No space for anything and anyone else.

Mother Yèlen asks for her attention. She wants her loneliness. Martyna doesn't know that her presence keeps Yèlen out; and Mary knows as well that a life without Martyna, without her irritating destructive power, could be a lagoon without a dam. Martyna can keep Yèlen away. Mary cannot let her discover about this power. It could be a real disaster – Martyna would crush Mary once and for all with her freak possessiveness.

Yèlen is everywhere, constantly.

Inside the walls, inside the floor and up there, inside the ceiling. If she were the house's blood, she would gush out wherever they scratched the walls.

And if there were a hole in the walls, into which Mary could stick her head, she would see her mother floating in the void, proud of her anorexia, soiling the enamel of her smile with black splashes of death.

DAVID, THE WHITE GUY: THURSDAY, 22TH OF JULY, 9 P.M.

A bottle of Negroamaro wine, pretty sour, is an accessory to a depressed Martyna as she toasts alone to her birthday. In the background, the band Kiss play in the living room – for the hundredth time – the album *Destroyer.*

"I wanna destroy her," Martyna mutters, chugging wine and spitting poison. She'd like to destroy Mary, tear her apart. That two-tone feeling for her isn't clear at all. It's quite like happy sadness, seductive repulsion. Dark Mary doesn't love her anymore, and she wants to get free – she knows. But it's too late, now, for both of them. That's why Martyna hates her, with all her hatred dripping from her mouth, down her neck. Usually, whenever Martyna is infused with rage, her photo creativity reaches levels of dramatic beauty. Recently, she discovered that with Photoshop's selective color editing, working on the neutral range palette, she can give her digital shots a delicate veil of blue, typical of Cibachrome film. Now, however, working wouldn't do any good. Martyna couldn't feel any good vibe, not even watching at her Dark Mary gallery. Her lover's complete cerulean bareness, the folds of her fragile skin. Nothing of Mary's could give Martyna any pleasure. Mary freezes Martyna's brain, making her inactive and useless, an unproductive and sterile idiot, just like any human being lacking creativity. This apathy, spawned by barrenness, suggests the true master in their relationship is the little DJ, and not the other. A thorn of pain and madness; this is their union, no way out. They are different, so much they could be sisters. But Martyna won't think she has mistaken good sex for love – never. Her story with Matthew was something else entirely. He was completely insane, but at least he wanted her, all to himself.

"Here we go. Martyna, get close and touch her," Matt told her as he spread the legs of a dead woman. They were in the mortuary. "I want you to kiss her," he said, starting to rub the cold meat of the corpse's vagina. "Right here."

"Matthew. Please, that makes me sick," Martyna replied, full of horror. That jerk couldn't know that her mother, Tamsen, forced her into incestuous oral sex when she was a little girl.

"You're not allowed to talk like that," Matt said.

That was Martyna's first experience with necrophilia – when she found out what the problem was with her boyfriend. That guy was as weird as he was charming. Now she knew why. Before going to the funeral home, Matt had driven her to a Henry Rollins Band gig. In that pub, they had drunk a lot of beer, then a bump of coke. She was only a heavy metal novice, loved the dark trend, walked around in graveyards by night and read dozens of novels about the supernatural. And then, the chance to visit the real lab of a funeral home – an exciting chance, better than anything. Matt was her dark superhero. But soon, and too late, she discovered the kind of confidence her boyfriend had with the flesh of corpses.

"The dead are wonderful to look at," he told, caressing Martyna. "They aren't different than us."

"They're not alive, Matt. You cannot touch them." Watching at the dead woman with the tinnitus from the Rollins gig was a chilling match.

"Did you really say I can't?" Matt replied, sneaking with his hand between Mrs. Sara's dead thighs. The woman naked on the table. "She likes it. As you see, she isn't complaining," Matt explained, spreading open her labia majora, and then sticking two fingers inside the barren orifice. It made a harsh, filthy sound. Matt masturbating the dead.

She remembers that slimy sound. The moment was weird and sick, so she tried to focus on Sara's quiet face. Martyna stared at her peaceful facial expression in the shadow, as Matthew vigorously plunged her cold birth canal. Suddenly, a strong dizziness dunked her brain. She was going to faint. For a second, she believed the woman on the table was only sleeping. Martyna sensed her alive: that was the crucial moment when death contaminated her mind. She'd made a living woman out of that dead thing, and then an ordinary carnal target.

"What are you waiting for, Martyna?" Matt asked, as he smelled the fingers he used to work the woman. "What are you thinking?"

"Uh… what?"

"Now I've warmed her up for you. I want you to kiss her, honey."

"No. I can't."

"Come on, my love. You can do it. Look at me." Matthew leaned down on the corpse. He slowly, languishingly kissed the lifeless opening between the stiff legs. Lifted his head and smiled at Martyna. "I'm not jealous," he said.

"This is disgusting lunacy," she protested.

"Let's share the taste of a kiss on this flesh, Martyna. Nobody in the whole world could ever say they've done anything like that."

She didn't want to kiss the dead woman's genitalia. But she did.

Matt made her do it. He grabbed her hair and pushed her head down.

Martyna's mouth ended up on the woman's pussy, living lips glued to dead ones, flesh and saliva. She could only grumble her dismay. He was high, and the hot situation was stirring his repressed furies. He rammed her head, many times, to keep her kissing between those purple, cold thighs. And as she kissed the dead with disgust and tears, Matt undressed her and took her virginity with rage and no pleasure. Then he hit the girl and left her unconscious on the floor. In the company of other bodies waiting to be washed, dressed, blessed, and put into their coffins.

When she awoke, Martyna found herself locked inside the corpse lab, in the dark. She screamed, until her mouth spat up blood from her throat. Everywhere she moved, she bumped into somebody sleeping the death. At some point, wandering in search of the light switch, she started to believe those unsteady bodies were colliding with her as they walked around in the gloom with aimless steps. After crying and screaming to exhaustion, she dropped on the ground, assaulted by anguish and by the sense of the abyss. Then, her mind turned off.

It started working again in the Pennsylvania forest. In a worse, tragicomic nightmare.

What a fucking birthday.

Dark Mary DMj is out, playing her records for Radio Rock Beach, Ostia Lido; out of Rome. Martyna is tired of chasing and stalking her. Maybe letting Mary think she is free to work can be sweeter, soothing, after all; letting her go out without the feeling to be in a cage. Martyna likes to imagine Mary sad for not seeing her lover in the crowd as usual; not seeing her checking out everybody who gets too close to Mary for an autograph, an interview, or a selfie. There must be something like three thousand dancing people and perhaps she's feeling alone, without her Martyna.

2,503 people, actually. The night is an adrenaline overload, and the show isn't even started.

Dark Mary DMj asked for pink lights for her new set, bulked up with a lot of punk classics. She wants to make that night unforgettable, and leave a deep mark in her fans' hearts. Mary wants to be shocking, tonight, acid pink, and she wants to become the color itself. She senses she's that color, today, a kind of magenta – not loved at all by her darkish metal fellows; that would be pure taunt, perfect for the incoming DJ set this tense, moist night.

The moment has come. DJ Armandino introduces Dark Mary from the radio station, on a tower with the main console, and he commands a pink lightning bolt, a magenta abyss into which the most powerful deejay Rome has ever known enters.

The crowd welcomes Mary with stadium uproar.

This is not a dance night.

This is an actual rock star concert.

Dark Mary isn't someone who plays records to make people dance. She *does* music. She *is* music. In the decadent sexuality of the sonic hurricane spilling out of Mary's wrists. Dark Mary is a fetish, an icon, a living religion.

From the top of the DJ tower, DMj turns into an alien, dipped in fluorescent fluid inside a sound tank ready to take off.

It all begins with Dead Can Dance's "Frontier" from their '84 debut album. Martyna hates that song because to her it sounds just like a wacko *tarantella* in ternary time. To Martyna, four-bar fundamentalist, that's pure heresy. To Mary, instead, "Frontier" is perfect to tell the world the despair caused by horrible love, a romance pleasant like retching, and linear like electroshock – perfect to destroy oneself with antidepressants and then to starve in a sanitarium bed.

The following songs are a waterfall from hell. Marilyn Manson's "The Beautiful People," Solitary Experiments' "Rise and Fall," Rammstein's "Haifish." Then, Mary breaks the run with a sudden funk-turn: Nine Inch Nails' "The Hand that Feeds," and going faster with Megadeth's "Dread of the Fugitive Mind," Ozzy's "11 Silver," Warrior Soul's "Let's Get Wasted," Guns N' Roses' "Shotgun Blues," Billy Idol's "Super Overdrive," White Wizzard's "40 Deuces." Funny-pausing with "Milk" by Anthrax, and the DJ set starts again beating hard with "Conjure the Mass" by Cauldron, "Killers "by Motorhead, "Feel Good Hit of the Summer" by Queens of the Stone Age, "Cok in my Pocket" by Iggy Pop & The Stooges, "Madhouse" by Uzi, and "Territorial Pissings" by Nirvana. Until the end, burning everything down with the mammoth "Bodies" by Sex Pistols, a live version from the *Filthy Lucre* reunion album.

Close to the speakers, the sand shakes and jumps at the hard metal wave, as though Godzilla were jogging on the asphalt of the Caio Duilio coastal road.

In this moment of massive rock earthquaking, Dark Mary becomes an absolute goddess.

Martyna thinks about her. Perhaps, as soon as her DJ set is over, Mary will grab the money, jump into the car and rush home with a fantastic present for her. Just like she did last year. First and last time.

She showed up wearing a tight-fitting latex suit. Low-cut dress, down to butt and pubis, thin harness on her small breasts. At her feet, high heels with leather-laced sandals, golden clasps, blue nail paint. Loose hair. To make the surprise perfect, Mary had done her makeup herself, without using a mirror. So her face was now decorated with nervous, inaccurate marks that disfigured her in a lovely way.

Mary had brought her a large bunch of thirteen roses made of human flesh on barbed wire stems. She had chatted up a she-male prostitute on Palmiro Togliatti Street near the eastern railway and an old slaughterhouse. She had killed and skinned the she-male in the darkness of a dirt road somewhere in the abandoned industrial park, where faceless customers were doing their best with other whores. Mary had sliced up tender ribbons from the belly of the corpse, thanks to a straight-bladed knife, and rolled them around the iron thorns of the wire, with the living red flesh on the outside. She had whittled the bloody roses to make the blossoms uneven and curly, like petals. The bunch of living dead flowers was still pouring blood as Mary handed the bouquet to Martyna. Back then she loved her. She had to kill for that gift; she had to work on a corpse to make art like that.

That was love.

Mary gave the flowers to Martyna, piercing the flesh of her hands with the metal thorns of the stems. Martyna took her present and kissed her, pushing her tongue inside Mary's throat and licking her teeth and face, eyes and ears too, pressing the roses between their chests. Kissing each other, they ended up in bed, mixing wounds and blood with breasts and barbed wire as tears and tongues washed their skins and souls like a flood. From the iBook, Dead Can Dance's "Enigma of the Absolute" was playing in a loop across the soft light of scattered candles. Martyna went under, and Mary rode her while undressing and offering herself to her nails, bites, everything. Rubbing their vaginas one against the other, clits and libs lubricated with internal fluid and the bloody squeezed flowers, the two of them began to shake and hit each other in scissors position while they ate the dead flesh still on the spiky stems, and repeating a million times *I love you*. Until even the last candle melted.

Now Martyna wants to play that song again, hear it again.

The slow arpeggio, in mystic gentleness, of a lonely guitar introduces the warm, sepulchral voice of Brendan Perry, his fancy accent and tender speech over timpani and cello, the elegiac singing.

Martyna sets an "Enigma" loop from *Spleen and Ideal* in the iTunes library. She tries to give an impressionist meaning to her Negroamaro bender, keeping in mind a grim project to celebrate this night.

Big scissors are on the night table beside the bed.

Martyna is weeping. This time for real. That song is so damn bonded to her sweetest memories with Dark Mary. It seems another life, like watching oneself in a movie. Frames run in front of her eyes and that's life. The motion picture is a window on a dream. Dreams move in an aquarium, beyond its glass, which has become opaque with age and neglect. This side, in front of the running images, the viewer stays in a lair of graphite dust and loneliness, a place where everybody's at the mercy of their own mind.

David, though. He's inside his terrarium. He has a life. He's ill, with the flu, so he must stay shut-in and warm for a while. Damn piece of shit. Dark Mary only loves that reptile, maybe more than herself.

"What the fuck does she see in that stinky tube of shit?"

Martyna just can't keep Mary out of her mind, picturing what she'd never want: her little DMj in a stranger's arms, a woman kissing her, someone who dares put her mouth where only Martyna should. When she did that to Mrs. Sara, the dead woman, her dismay was immense and awfully delightful, and she was little more than a child back then. The choking imprinting of cerebral unstoppable pleasure, as unstoppable as the advance of Death. A form of degenerative love that leads you deeper and deeper, in the worst darkness. The same way the flesh corrupts, rots, and finally disintegrates into mute dirt. But this pleasure isn't meant for everybody, and Dark Mary must remain hers and only hers. Loving Mary is like a contagious, aggressive venereal disease; once made contact, you're not free anymore, and you'll spread it everywhere and forever. And the dulling Dark Mary addiction is a paradise that could be extended like an epidemic, under an infinite sunset of compulsive obsession, mind-blowing jealousy, eternal and utter slavery to flesh in the antimatter of love – where everything is dark, painful, unhappy, unlucky, and predestined to the quickest death.

Martyna must keep Mary for herself, must renew her supremacy and mutilate any purpose of separation. Dark Mary doesn't love her; that's why she has to be compelled.

Absolute runs across the musty air of the house. David seems to sleep. Martyna gets naked, letting her clothes drop at her feet. Her pubis is shaved. She likes herself. She slides open the lid of the terrarium. She takes out the albino python with her hands, and carries him to the bedroom. There is a white, low light waiting for them, blank walls and old yellow-ivory wallpaper, and a cold bottle of Batida de Coco. Martyna lays David in the middle of the bed. She looks at him. The snake lazily moves on the blanket, and he sneezes. One, two, three sips of Batida – Martyna's stomach becomes a fireball. Her brain, instead, a bubble. She lies down on the bed. Then, throws up on the floor, soiling the wall, too. She swears and curses Mary. She cleans up with the blanket, then grabs the snake who was trying to creep down the bed. The Dead Can Dance are still playing "Enigma" inside a no-way-out maze. Martyna forces David to come over and stay on her naked body, to give him all the warmth she can, from feet to head, for all his smooth length. Martyna grabs David's head and brings his snout close to her nose. She stares at the snake's eyes and wonders what he sees through those thin pupils, what Mary could see in them. With his tongue, David tastes Martyna's damp breath, while summer heat is making the night boil, covering her skin with the sweat of unhappy desires. The snake is cold and sleek as he shifts his mobile ribs as internal legs slowly move on the moist human skin. He likes the woman's warmness, just like she loves that honest caress. Nobody has been so gentle with her since Dark Mary stopped loving and coddling her. The snake coils between the woman's legs, looking just between her legs for the spot to steal the most warmth.

Watching at that living, white-shining tube over her body is so arousing for Martyna. "You already did it with her. Didn't you, little asshole?"

David sticks out his tongue, catching the alcoholic breath of the woman. "C'mon, creep. Come and wish me happy birthday," Martyna mutters, lost in coconut rum numbness, pushing the snake's head against her mons pubis. David seems to refuse being pressed on her flesh creases. She recalls when Matt shoved her against Mrs. Sara's vagina. She must do the same, now. They call it revenge.

Martyna can't accept being rejected even by a living fledgling-eating tube of shit like that.

"No. Please, no," she whispers, crying and grinding her teeth.

She gets angry, so she spits on her hand, lubes herself, and shoves that little head inside her hole, moaning as it's brutally broadened. David's head is now inside Martyna's cunt. The python darts back like a spring, trying to get free in vain while Martyna's iron grip pushes him much harder, making the animal go a little deeper. David doesn't waste any more time; he opens his mouth and blindly bites.

"Fuck!" Martyna arches on the bed, electrocuted by massive pain. She squirts blood while David keep biting her uterus. Grabbing the scissors, Martyna hits the snake, again and again, piercing the bed. David stops moving, drowning in blood. His white coils slow until they freeze in the red puddle between Martyna's legs. The woman drops the scissors on the floor. She sighs, and moans. Her heart beats loud.

Dead Can Dance go on playing their song.

The bathroom halogen lamp is perfect.

It's 10:12 p.m..

David is dead, and swinging between Martyna's legs like a uterine tail.

Blood runs down, twisting around the snake's white scales. A can't-miss photograph.

"Fuck off," Martyna cries with rare enthusiasm.

She already has the title for that picture: *e-reptile.* A great title for a masterwork.

She grabs her Sony cam. While pain throbs its deaf advance, she begins to take a heap of pictures she already sees turned into vintage Polaroid via Photoshop tricks.

"A snake-eating cunt; a cunt-eating snake."

Martyna takes almost sixty photos, raw mode. With a little blur, they're going to have a real Seventies appeal. This will be like that Newyorker mortuary kiss to Mrs. Sara: nobody in the whole world could emulate such an idea. Only her *Decoroner* will have it. "Nobody'll dare do fucking stuff like this. This is the real deal ... shit, this is photo-reportage."

The trickles of blood are beginning to glue her thighs to the dead snake. The pics will show an incomparable testimony, an effect that only human blood can sort. After taking the right number of shots, Martyna puts her Sony away and takes her knife.

Time to extract David.

Step number one. It's necessary to cut the snake's head, leaving a stretch of its body, long enough to be grasped and pulled out with ease.

Step number two. A rightful dose of oxycodone and a sniff of popper. The drugs suggest the ultimate, supreme idea.

Step number three. It's 11:00 p.m. The Sony cam is on the bottom of the bathtub, upon an old book. Program: a set of self-timer shots with twelve-second intervals. Close to the cam, an enlarging mirror where Martyna will follow the maneuver details. Needle and nylon fishing line ready on the tub edge, wire cutters, straight-bladed knife, and a retractor. Tools she knows well from many of her masterworks.

It's 11:02 p.m..

Martyna climbs into the tub. Just in time: the opioid has almost anesthetized her whole lumbar area. Her legs can't hold her anymore. She spreads them, on either side of the cam lens to get a complete frame of the operation. The Sony lies on three books, raised from the bottom of the tub. A gushing, out-of-control jet of pee washes the part of the snake still inside Martyna, vanishing into the tub drain after soaking the pages of the book under the camera. Martyna laughs. Then, she starts the shooting session.

It's 11:10 p.m.

Using the same blade that cut David, Martyna opens her taint. Pain is far away, almost absent. She can have control. She can watch what happens in the mirror, at the same time getting aroused by the camera watching her. Her brain splits as well as she opens up two new, red-pouring lips from her vagina to her anus. Her hand doesn't tremble. She has no mercy, no hesitation.

"Oh, yeah," she whispers, feeling the mute call of the flesh opening under the blade. Martyna is losing blood. No fear. Warm red oil. Skin cannot feel, but the mirror can tell. She's so proud of herself. In some way, that selfie-surgery is the continuation of the ancient cunnilingus at Matt's funeral home. A vertical, deadly cut across time and space. A super-divine mark.

Martyna chucks the blade aside, then inserts the retractor to keep the fresh cut wide open. She falls madly in love with the inside of herself. She only regrets, right now, that she cannot kiss her open flesh and get drunk with that madness. What a pity. Blood pours like mud, and looking in the mirror Martyna quickly realizes this is not the right way to extract David at all. She has prepared all the tools but maybe she should have read some medical book before beginning. "Shit."

She closes the retractor and put it near the blade. There's blood everywhere. The hems of the wound slowly close. Blood stops spilling by itself. It's a matter of seconds.

Now Martyna makes an incision from navel to pubis bone. Then, she spreads the wound with the retractor, as much as she can. The blade has gone really deep. Her abdominal wall, now slashed, lets her bowels come out. She moves them apart and goes on cutting her insides with the knife, until she digs up David's snout, his jaws shut on her cervix. The white of his head shines on the crucible of blood. She must move the camera to capture that precious detail. Snap. Snap. Snap. The cam portrays everything. Martyna uses the wire cutter. She carves the snake head in several chunks. Then, it will be easily extracted. It's a work of patience. Luckily, a snake mouth is a wishbone system, so it's simple to destroy and split the jaws.

It's 11:22 p.m.

Martyna quickly shreds David's head. "Crip crip, crip," she sings along, reproducing the sound of the wire cutter on the dead animal. The noise of bones crumbled by the tool creates a rhythm with the digital camera snapping. Martyna takes the head slivers out of her flesh. Her blood is mixed with the python's. She's pretty wide open, and with her fingers she can go deep and clean the wound of all the snake's snout pieces. Working on the rear of her uterus proves harder. She has to pull and hack both sides of David's lower jaw. The sound of tearing flesh is devastating, but the woman won't stop. She's slashing her own birth tunnel in a river of blood. The books, on which the camera rests, are completely drenched.

David is completely out of Martyna, now. His neck and chunks form a line on the edge of the tub. The rounded surface is a graveyard of bloody bricks of dead meat.

The woman can relax for a while. After shoving her bowels back in through the belly wound, she rests her head back. One more sniff of popper to suture herself until the camera clock displays it's 11:49 p.m. The film has captured her hands muddy with plasma and fat tissue. But the sewing has gone well.

At twenty-three past midnight Martyna has a short nap inside the tub. The surgery has been portrayed in 365 raw shots. Just some more pics of the tools and the dead pieces on the edges of her bloodied thighs, too, and of the blood splattered everywhere.

Martyna has another ketamine sniff to be able to get to the bedroom and give herself over to sleep. Maybe a dive into a comatose state, to party with some sublime near-death experiences.

THAT'S ALL, CREEPERS

Dark Mary is in the bathroom. Her flight case with MacBooks and headphones is on the floor, among pale atolls of blood and a chaos of stains. Surgery tools covered in plasma are on the tub edges. The perfect night at Ostia, Radio Rock Beach, is in total contrast to what Mary sees and does not understand. Blood everywhere, the knife, wire cutter and the Sony camera in that room of butchery.

Confused, bloody footprints leave the room after wandering round and round, coming from inside the tub. Clear blood mix with brown blood. The tub is all smeared in purple and rusty plasma, slices of snake where only a few days ago Martyna washed her with so much love and tenderness.

Inside the bathtub, the beheaded python lies on his back. All around, shatters of his head. The memory of him alive seems to date a long time back.

One last streamlet of blood slowly goes down the round edges, trickling below the belly of the tub and on the floor. That dripping of sadness and misery is thundering.

Mary collects some pieces of her beloved's head. She studies them, as though she could rebuild the animal. Giving him life again.

"David."

Mary is crying a sea of tears, her knees against the bathtub. Blood climbs her feet and legs like a relentless ivy. Tears wash down, diluting the blood on which David's remains lay abandoned. Mary's moaning has a metallic reverb from the tub. Something heavy suddenly flies overhead.

"Go away."

Mary starts eating David. She eats and cries.

At first, the shreds of his head. Then, his body, her sharpened nails tearing pieces of meat. Her crying goes down her throat together with the dead food. Blood trickling down her chin and neck soaks her black dress to her belly. Dark Mary undresses, leaving on only her black cotton panties. Then she takes David's last section and, squeezing it, washes herself over with blood from the head down. After that, she uses the dripping snake stump as a brush to paint her face red; and then her neck, arms, back, and legs. There's no music that could fit this moment to be imprinted in memory as a special attachment to David's death.

Dark Mary has been pink.

She's red now.

She's inside-out.

"I burn."

Mary throws up.

Her regurgitation is roaring, amplified by the tub. She stays there, bent on the floor. She vomits again because she hasn't chewed the stringy snake meat well. Her cavernous scream ends with viscid bumps on the tiles. She seems to have swallowed a bunch of cotton threads, or talcum powder. Her stomach overturns, pushing out clots of acidic meat and blood. David doesn't want to stay inside her. He wants to stay on her skin. He comes out in pulp.

The raw mass on the floor sparkles with the anger of an inglorious death. The blood begins to cake on Mary's skin, pulling in every direction.

"I haven't finished yet."

Martyna hears Mary's guttural noises, but she can't react.

She's motionless, naked, in the same position and same spot Mary was for two days. Ketamine has sent her to coma.

Her blue eyes are open wide and see. Her ears can hear. But Martyna's mind is elsewhere, derailed toward nowhere. The light from the bathroom is growing in the hall, ever more blinding, dissolving the eternal shadows that reign inside this house. A white, brilliant light. It's like a globe of fire rolling across the hall to enter the bedroom and run Martyna over. Inside the lower levels of consciousness, Martyna knows well that she's just started her first near-death experience.

All her nerves reply to the blinding blaze. She's able to half-close her eyelids to bear the vastness of the light, even if the light is only inside her mind. A sudden lightning flash make her eyes shut, but a globe of white fire remains impressed inside. When she opens them again, the globe of fire is now on the wall, in front of the bed, flaming there and thin like a wind-shaken spider web.

Martyna flies with raven wings, ascending toward the ceiling. She's really doing that. She can even see herself lying on the bed. Her body has sutures on her belly and between her legs. She realizes she can't fly, so she begins to drop to the floor. She moves her arms to hold back the air. She rises again and flies straight into the center of the white fire on the wall. She goes across, beyond it, into the bathroom, her shoulder brushing against the ceiling. She flies above Dark Mary on her knees, sees her crying over the pulp of her poor David.

Mary senses her presence and growls – *go away* – with her usual cold rage.

Martyna turns back and flies toward the fire on the wall, blinded as she looks at the blaze. She loses control. She falls once again. The slam is soft, on grass.

The blaze is spreading. It has become a magnificent afternoon sky above the Ancient Appian Way of Rome, not far from the

Catacombs of Cecilia Metella. Martyna is there, now.

Hectares of grass, plane trees, and cypresses all around Roman stones, marble bas-reliefs and broken columns, tree-lined secondary avenues toward luxury private properties, vestiges. It's freaking unbelievable, but a little path, Capo di Bove Street, which ends into the Ancient Appian Way, comes from an offshoot of Sproul Forest, Pennsylvania.

Martyna moves onto the green path, and soon she can see in the distance Goehn's house in the woods. Yes, him, Matt's old friend. The wind blows hard, and his door slams and squeaks.

Somewhere a beast is screaming, roaring; it bellows, it chirps. The beast is chasing someone who's yelling and crying out for help, and who falls to the ground to be attacked from behind.

Martyna can see everything that's happening.

The beast slaughters him with claws, with bites, turning his flesh into a carnival of pieces, only kept together by resilient nerves and tendons like the strings of a broken puppet moved by rage and madness.

Martyna cries out, even though she doesn't recognize Matthew as the victim.

The beast turns aside and spots Martyna. It sees her fear. Martyna must run. She stumbles on the stones, gets back up and tries to flee across the fields instead of going toward the city center of Rome along the Ancient Appian. The beast roars behind her – it has already found her, thanks to a flawless sense of smell.

Martyna looks back. That beast is none other than her mother Tamsen. The woman is now a colossal manticore made of pale wood. She walks on four legs, yelling and making her medieval snap-fit joints squeak on iron cylindrical linchpins. More than an animal, she is a float. Her tongue rolls out her mouth, opened in a crazy grin, spreading all over her dirty, salty drool. Her eyes are headlamps of treachery, adorned with white and green paint. Her hair is rays of plaits bunched up with bitumen. It looks like a Chinese sanitarium dragon.

"So, c'mon, kiss it," Tamsen cries in a fury. She carries a black pope on her hollow, bloody back.

Martyna is forced to stop, and keep watching.

Tamsen turns right on her creaking paws, stepping on the Ancient Appian, toward the city. She's no longer interested in Martyna. The black pope is blessing and crossing, murmuring in Latin. Martyna realizes the man is her father. Dressed in white, he hawks up phlegm and wipes his mouth with his mozzetta. Behind him there are two eunuchs, who swing medieval flails to keep flies and other flying insects away from the pope's holy shoulders.

Here Matthew is, at last. He follows the manticore. Undressed, he drags a big wooden cross full of nails that wound him every step. The longest nail pierces him through his nape, coming out his mouth through the teeth, twisting his neck every time the cross sways on his back and weak legs. A pack of wolves, black like peat, keep watch and push him, forcing him with quick bites to walk toward death. The animals are curves of soot, moving stains, their paws blurry and confused as they rapidly move. Their tails and heads are unsteady spots where white sparks reveal eyes and fangs. They howl and snarl, darting out from the pack and smelling the dirt; then back again to lose themselves among their counterparts. Martyna cannot tell anything precise about the shape and number of wolves hunting down her Matthew.

The man goes on, weaker and weaker, because the animals rip his muscles from his legs, bite after bite. Their fangs tear strips of skin away as they fight for the best piece. Matt cannot stop. They pounce on him, anchoring with their claws to his back. They howl into his ears the direction he must take. The funeral march stirs up the dust. Finally, Matthew makes eye contact with Martyna. He tries to call her, but a wolf leaps at his throat and chokes his voice. Matt's eyes explode, so he cannot watch anymore. The animal gets back to its pack, howling and snarling with the others as though the man were the last sheep of its flock. Matt goes on, along the Ancient Appian Way with his wooden cross, straight down to the horizon where the sun is burning down everything.

Sunlight grows, making the scene of Martyna's vision disappear. But this is only a change. The light becomes white, now projected by a human body.

Martyna now sees her shining-bright Dark Mary.

The petite girl is standing on the dark waters of the bathtub.

She's naked, her feet in the calm, dirty liquid. Her milk-white skin seems radioactive as it illuminates the bathroom. The pulsation of her light follows her breathing, and when it's less intense Martyna begins to see a crowd of young naked people around Mary. Those guys are watching her, adoring, crying, and burning with desire. The closest of them move even nearer around Mary, jumping and dancing with no music and no sound, though the air vibrates at an invisible force. As they are about to touch Mary, the light source, they are slashed one by one, head to belly, but there are no blades, only sharpened rays of light. The adoring dancers fall in slices at the others' feet. Flesh, bowels, and blood melt on the floor in a swamp, warm and dead.

Gracefully, Mary turns around and spreads her legs. She bends her knees and leans with her ass over the bathtub. With her fingers, she opens her pussy, then she pisses a golden jet over the red human sea. Her urine is fluorescent on the meat swamp, and it lightens the surface among strands of grease and a bush of dead veins.

The human soup boils. From the foamy glow, a shape emerges. That's Matthew. He's enveloped in a sort of amniotic paste. He's rising from death.

Still standing on the tube, Dark Mary welcomes him in her arms. She helps him climb in the black water with her. She embraces him, accepts him; freeing him of the paste, she caresses him. Matthew opens his eyes and watches in the eyes of the woman. He can breathe deeply, quenching his thirst for life. On his back, his skin inflates until it breaks, and a pair of wings comes out that shines with superb candor. The crowd of faithful all around keeps dying under the blade of light, hacked to slices, giving their limbs to the swamp of meat. The level of blood is rising, almost up at the tub edges, but the two lovers inside the bathtub seem not to care about it. Mary makes Matt turn around, then she grabs his wings and begins to pluck them. She pulls feathers and plumes away until the wings are bare and peeled and riddled with red holes where the quills sank. Matthew raises the wings over his head and clutches Mary, digging their naked ends into her neck. Mary's eyes open wide. She holds Matt tighter, body against body. At the contact, their skin burns in corrosion. Then, Mary pushes Matt away, and their exposed hearts swing between their chests, melted into one another, pulsating together as one. Mary puts on her headphones and plugs the jack to the beating muscles. She begins to dance at the cardiac rhythm. Dark Mary lays her hands on Matthew, and her sharpened nails open his head from the forehead, like peeling fruit. Matthew still stands, but his body shakes as Mary tears out his frontal lobes. She puts these warm, pink morsels in her mouth, and licks her fingers when she's full, and the crowd in the bathroom has totally died. Matt falls in the dark water, his lifeless, naked wings leaning on the tub edges like the long legs of a dead spider. Mary needs to clean herself. She climbs off the tub and goes toward the curtain. She forcefully pulls the cloth until it comes down together with its metal rod.

Mary picks up the rod and goes into the bedroom.

The vision ends with Mary entering the bedroom, holding the iron pole.

When Martyna opens her real eyes, she sees Mary standing in front of her.

Burning with rage.

THE FILTHY FOUR BASTARDS, PART II: FIRST NIGHT OF FULL MOON, 31ᵀᴴ OF JULY

Nine p.m..

Alfredo Vanacura is smoking a pipe at the window of his flat, enjoying the sweet tobacco and the fresh air of the Jewish ghetto.

But he is also staring at the attic of the old building across the street. An obsession that's been haunting him for years. One out of many others filling his mind.

When he was a child, Alfredo used to run into a boy his age, always and everywhere. He met him by chance. He wasn't his friend and he would have never wanted to be. Without any reason at all, Alfredo hated him, despised him. The whole family of that boy disgusted him – large and rowdy, underdressed and rude folks. They had four or five neurotic, stinky dogs; and nobody could say who was the least human of that pack. Alfredo couldn't stand bumping into him all the time: at the elevator door, at the front door, around the neighborhood, at the bar, at the postal office or any shop. He saw him going out as he was going in and vice versa. And that pinwheel of random encounters was becoming ever more apparent and distressing. Alfredo hated his idiotic face, his half-mast eyes, the rough overgrown-animal voice – in awful contrast with his faggot outfit. At fifteen, Alfredo began to feel superstitious and touch his balls whenever he saw him because he thought that boy was a jinx. That had been the first in a long series of persecutions creeping inside Alfredo's mind. The first he remembers, at least. All the following ones would spin around his feelings of inferiority. His later enemies, except for some people – no doubt, less dangerous – became sexual diseases, the fear of being cheated of his money, cockroaches, strangers, and the massive crime front. More than outlaws, hundreds of varied things then became the kidnappers of his psyche: a displaced book, viral infections, rotten food, the fixed residue of bottled water. Little fights against himself in the portrait of daily life, uncountable drip-feeds to anesthetize, all in all, his ultimate enemy: the fear of being marginalized.

That attic window is the sick eye watching his mousy life. Shut for years, burnt by the sun, puffed by rain and black with dust.

Roller shutter eternally closed, the house cannot be seen by anyone. It's lonely. Summer is the lonely season. It's all about the temporary mass of holidaymakers. But one dinner at a pizzeria is enough; there'll be at least someone who feels lonely. The more crowded the public place – restaurants, pubs, music arenas – the higher the spiritual fever will be, if you know you're a walking dead confronted with others who live their success or a mediocre life.

"But ... wait a moment," Alfredo says, frowning as he stares at the window. "Music arenas!" he says loudly. His pineal gland rings like a phone. Brain is calling the Marshal. Intuition bites like a tarantula.

Alfredo goes back to the *Scanners* dossier.

Priscilla, Roberto, Alberto, Valentina.

"The night they died, they'd all been at music shows."

It's late, but the Marshal really has to call that idiot Fildor. The pathologist has been strangely silent since their last meal at the *Obituary*. Despite the discovery of new bodies with no blood and no hearts – tramps, this time: a man and a woman, hidden among the bushes of San Lorenzo Park.

"Please, don't call me, Alfredo. I'm on vacation," Fildor answers. His voice quivers with tension. "I'm close to a breakdown."

"Vacation? Oh, man. Please, don't give up on me now. I think I have a lead to the killer and his beast. It's someone drawn to music arenas, concerts and such. We only have to follow the show calendar and –"

"Nonsense. You can't ... we can't win this battle, Marshal."

"Hey, mate. Don't you try to –"

The sound of the phone hanging-up, then the busy signal.

Heat and loneliness. Alfredo is washed over by an icy snow slide, and yet he keeps sweating.

"Oh, shit. Now I'm pissed."

Another glance at the window in front.

Alfredo takes his Beretta SB 92 pistol and goes out.

Dark Mary is still swallowing tears of bitterness.

Often, getting over a sickness doesn't bring relief, but a different kind of pain. Mary curses her own heart. It feels like having a cup of punishment inside her chest, full with the juice of poison berries. She preferred leaving Martyna alive. Killing her would have been too easy. That woman must suffer for what she's done to David. Coward and selfish as fitting to a corpse lover. She must pay in humiliation, for as long as possible. At last, Martyna has left home, taking away her little luggage, her huge wrathful jealousy, her pharisaic bipolar meanness.

So, Yèlen is free to invade the space left, feeding on the silence, pushing her branches inside Mary's mind, begging for alms of love – the affective cancer of the ones who play the victim's role to gain the world's attentions. However, better a mental worm than a coward in your home.

Dark Mary is alone, tonight.

David's pieces have been eliminated. Maybe he's already in Heaven, looking for an apple tree.

Tonight, a lot of fucking people could die.

The same night, Fildor's morgue lab.

Silence and tidiness everywhere.

It's 9:33 p.m., according to the Baume & Mercier at his wrist. The Marshal must call Fildor. He tries his mobile first, dialing his mate's number by heart.

360610895. He waits. Unavailable.

Maybe he's blocked my number.

Alfredo tried again from the lab phone. Unavailable.

He tries to call him at home.

Fildor does not answer.

Better take a look at the refrigerators.

The Marshal approaches and opens the steel doors. He finds all the *Scanners* guys: the ones called dry maggots and the others, with their heads exploded. Seeing those bodies cleaned and composed in their devastation is an unreal journey across surrealist necroscopy. The Prefect ordered that the victims' families must not be informed about their finding. *Scanners* must be covered up.

The Marshal realizes that the four bodies of the racetrack scene are missing.

Where are their bodies?

Something weird is definitely going on.

"Fildor is losing it," Alfredo says. Pretty worried. "This is getting out of hand."

The clairvoyant Marshal turns on Fildor's PC to look up the corpse log and perhaps find the missing ones. But he doesn't have the password.

Fuck. Fuck. Fuck.

Fildor's house. Close to the Coliseum, San Saba Street. Alfredo presses the door phone button. Nobody answers. Alfredo pushes again, for forty seconds. Nobody. Lights are off. *Maybe he's taken sleeping pills? Or he killed himself?* Alfredo calls Fildor's phone. No answer before getting cut off.

"I hope that jerk has gone to the lake. But why he didn't tell me?"

Dark Mary is ready. She knows where to go. She knows what lies ahead.

The smell of blood has led them here. The smell of blood is a railway ridden by her percipience.

White man, thirty. She has already seen him; that guy approached her a few hours ago, during her DJ set.

He's on the ground, among cypresses at the Casilina route park, formerly the Centocelle Airport. The man's body is sort of like the slaughtering manifesto, but he hasn't died nor fainted yet. He floats on a lake of blood. Dark Mary must be careful where to step. That blood could be contagious; she must stay clean. Nobody around. Nobody should have seen. The man lies on the ground, burning on a bed of hurt that crashes his mind.

He's sliced from head to toe, as though he were in a rain of knives. He cannot stand. He falls every time he tries. His muscles, drawn out from his skin, are also torn by bites, and they drip their last, shy tears of blood. His heart is giving up. The man sees Dark Mary. Better, he recognizes her. He cannot make sense of what a celebrity like her may be doing in an absurd place like that, in front of him.

"Would you sign my picture of you, please?" the man asks with his warped smile. His facial muscles pull ripped lips, baring teeth submerged in black plasma.

Piotr is nervous.

Since his three friends died in the racetrack parking lot, his life has completely changed. Before they died – and he still cannot remember *how* – they really were four busy bastards. A lot of beer, some little thievery, and sometimes they raped prostitutes around town. It's so hard to end up in jail, in Italy, for that kind of recreation. They just had to hang out at some community center, hit on some drunk chick and screw her. But things have deeply changed now, and Piotr hates everybody and everything. Except for beer bottles, thefts, and scuffles, he has no friends anymore. Over all, he has no longer a place to go. He doesn't want to start working as a bricklayer, or slave away at potato fields. He doesn't want to do shit. Those friends, who used to keep him busy with stealing and screwing all around, are gone. He's alone now. Alone with his stupid brain. Even *they* told him he was an idiot, but because they loved him.

It's 11:20 p.m.

Piotr is loitering around the community center near the ex-SNIA, the old textile industrial area built in the early 20s and abandoned during the 50s. Now it is a dead city hosting illegals from Africa, hidden by wild vegetation and rotten cabins. The area is surrounded by an eight-foot-tall wall of old bricks and reinforced concrete, barred iron doors, rusty gates, barbed wire.

The community center is always a quiet place, though. There's a party, tonight, with a lot of multicolored people, a mountain of pot, musicians, and jugglers.

Maybe he had too much kebab. His stomach is upside-down.

He must get away.

He's gonna puke.

He's thirsty.

Suddenly, he feels an incredible thirst.

And feels a growing rage rising inside him.

Thinking of his friends dead on the Renault at Capannelle racetrack upsets him, makes his neck veins burst, his fist clenching until the knuckles turn white.

"Hey, dude. Are you all right?" a Jamaican boy asks. A short hip-hop fellow with his pant crotch sagging close to the ground.

"Stay the fuck out. Fuck off, nigger," the Russian growls. "Fuckin jankee."

"Screw you, asshole," the Jamaican screams. He doesn't fear that Cyrillic behemoth. His insult is helped by a switchblade in a steady hand. A couple of compatriots come along, dangling. "Piss off," they say, shoving him. Other people get closer. Everybody against Piotr. "Get the fuck away. Is it clear, or you're a complete turd?" The short Jamaican with the blade seems to have many friends. They come running, ready to start up a mess for him. Piotr no longer has any friends to call for backup. That little dick has friends. There are no Russians at this fuckin' party. Nobody who can help Piotr, to teach those black dogs a lesson. That music, too. That music makes him mad; it gets into his head and gives him electric shocks. Those fucking people. Rage grows. He hears someone calling the police.

"Fucking shit. Fucking shit," Piotr sighs, running away, his palms shutting his ears. The young man runs out of the community center. He stands a few moments on the sidewalk of Prenestina Street. He takes a look all around as traffic makes an unbearable noise. The black guys watch the community center gate so that the drunk Russian doesn't get back in. They keep insulting and threatening him.

Piotr enters the park near the ex-SNIA. He walks along the narrow dirt alley that borders the San Lorenzo freight yard and the abandoned textile area. Some folks are even there, smoking, so Piotr can move unseen. Tonight, he's willing to kill someone, anyone.

Standing between palms and pine trees, the full moon seems to be watching at him – at Piotr, indeed. That circle of light in the sky pisses him off. It hammers his head without pause.

Stupid. Stupid. Stupid, the moon says. The satellite mirrors itself on the artificial lake, among the ruins of the industrial city, high grass and canes.

Water. Piotr needs water.

He's burning inside.

But it isn't rage anymore.

Suddenly, he feels the bones of his skull slide over one another, making the sound of an old wooden boat. His face is breaking up. He's frightened. What's happening to his face? He wants to call for help, but what comes out from his mouth is a strange and rough vocalization. In a language neither Russian nor Italian. He takes off his tank top, then he tries to tear apart – barehanded – the metal fence delineating the small cliff over the artificial pond. He gets wounded, of course, and he isn't strong enough to rip it. So he runs back and forth until he finds a gap, apparently used by someone to climb down toward the railway and the rotten buildings of ex-SNIA.

Piotr is drawn to the dark pool, already a Kasbah for tiger mosquitos. The lake spawns from an ancient underground aquifer that once gave origin to a malarial swamp. The insects attack Piotr, storming him with bites as he leans to drink at the shore. The moon torches his head, stronger than midday sun.

His stomach fills with dead water and maggots, and it squirms. Sudden retching hits like a whiplash over the rest of his body, and he begins to shake.

His bones tremble, and his flesh, as though wanting to fly away from the young man.

Piotr drops to his knees for the pain that beats his calves, thighs, belly. His spine bends, creaking, like a snake inside his back, making his ribs shift in waves while his face cracks to push out his nose. The shakes makes Piotr roar as his teeth shift in their alveoli, spilling blood.

The Russian watches his hands. His fingers curl with spasmodic, extreme tension. They want to grab, scratch, crush, strangle, tear. Piotr also wants to get naked. Naked in contact with the air, naked to the night. All the sounds of the woods get clearer, sneaky, and insolent to his ears – already tortured by his pulsating brain, by his heart that echoes in his mind and slams like a howitzer spraying blood over his flaming breath.

Feet sinking in the putrid shore.

Breath commanded by furious bellows.

Drool coming down foamy from the sides of his mouth.

Thirst. The internal fire makes him thirsty. Rage makes his throat dry.

Piotr screams. It's not water he wants, now.

He screams again and starts to run.

"Stop there!"

It's not the moonlight chasing him.

It comes from the flashlight of a shooting man.

First at the sky, then at his legs.

Piotr is shot, but he keeps running and grunting. He climbs the cliff, the grass, toward the metal fence.

The man shoots fire into his flesh.

Every hit is a nail piercing him. He must run away, but now he can only roll back down.

Other men come, and other flashlights.

They surround him.

Piotr tries to hide among the higher grass of a small decrepit building. He realizes he should stop running, otherwise those men will keep shooting nails of fire. Just a little relief to take a breath, to take shelter.

A Carabinieri patrol had been called in for a disturbance at the community center.

"Don't move!" Captain Salvatores says.

His agents aim beam of light at some strange creature's face, which screams and growls. And as another tries to get closer, the man-thing swings a downward blow with a hand. Long nails. His eyes reveal that he will skin the face off anybody who dares move another step.

Stuck with his back to the wall, he reaches around, hand flitting over the rough surface behind him, like he's searching for a hole, some means to escape.

"Stay still. Don't move," the Captain orders, certain the thing understands. "Stay still and nobody will shoot again." He pauses. Tension. His snarl. "Calm down."

No doubt, the guy under the flashlight beam is a man. But his skin is dark, spotted with furry patches. His neck makes a lump between his risen shoulders. His tongue moves between displaced teeth, and his breath is reminiscent of a gasping dog.

The face. His face is a big issue.

"Bring me a net and a tranquilizer gun," Salvatores orders. "Keep him at gunpoint."

They've never seen anything like this before. The eyes are lost in madness and they dart on either side of a baboon-like face.

An elongated nose smells the air.

Hectically.

What.

The fuck.

Is he?

Marcello was born in Rome. As a child, Father beats him, Mother comforts him. The seventies: with all these giant full-color posters in the streets, Sunday church, the tram around the city passing through the ancient Porta Maggiore, San Peter's dome, the schoolbag with Pinocchio's head, the secondary school at Augusto, his grandmother dying young, a holiday in Lampedusa, a rally with tear gas, gunfire across the old town during the Years of Lead, his very first girlfriend, his old father ignoring any grudge, a bunch of prostitutes at his service, his career as a judge, the hot days at the Cassazione Palace court, his arrest and the sentence for child abuse and exploitation, his last days as a homeless alone with a dog. Sixty seconds. Even the hereafter hasn't a minute to spare.

Father Sebastiano has just finished reading Marcello's heart. A brand new heart for his underground collection. The pale priest has read his stored memories, drinking them, putting his lips to an artery section of the still-beating muscle, like a cardiac bottle. That heart, as the others, pulsates and contracts open-cast, free from the chest that used to cage it, blowing in the priest's face stale air from inside atria and ventricles.

In the underground cellar, Sebastiano hangs the newcomer heart on the wire mesh. Together, with the others, it's a candidate for a great transplant project, something out of God's grace but necessary. Covered by a veil of electric light, Sebastiano watches over that little orchard of pulsing hearts for a while. Each beats in different time, in a unique, obscene group. That space – iron mesh, bricks, and living flesh. The porphyria-sick priest wonders if those hearts keep beating even when they're all alone in the dark, in the bowels of Rome, or if they stop while he's away and resume as he returns. There are no answers. Only faith. Sebastiano is a special man.

The Vatican has given him simple tasks. Which he uses as a front to hide the marvels that God has allowed him to see, to live, and to manage.

"I guess we have to keep on searching," Sebastiano says to Marcello's beating heart.

"A dog-man," Captain Salvatores whispers aboard the Penitentiary Police truck. Actually, he would have gone with *man-ape*, but the prisoner's deformed face reminds him too much of Proust, his white Bull Terrier.

Salvatores had earlier called Alfredo Vanacura. The ex-Marshal immediately joined them – putting on standby his search for Fildor – and is now looking at the paralyzed body tied to the stretcher with thick leather belts. The almost-man-almost-animal keeps his eyes open, staring at the vehicle hood.

"I can't believe ..." the Marshal says.

"What, Marshal?" Salvatores asks.

"I can't believe what I'm seeing, Captain," Alfredo says, lying.

Alfredo's sentence skillfully covers a thought that cannot be verbalized to ordinary people: *I can't believe we captured a werewolf.*

RAGE AGAINST THE SEX MACHINE: 2ᴺᴰ NIGHT OF FULL MOON, AUGUST THE 1ˢᵀ

The eastern bypass of the city runs parallel to a railway and a small savannah that ends at the Salaria route, also called Statale 4, which runs from Rome to the Adriatic Sea. Since time immemorial, the Salaria is the reign of the youngest prostitutes. They wait for customers from dawn until night, only wearing tight swimsuits – some totally naked – as if they were at the beach, or in a lap dance club.

The wolf isn't hungry. Its stomach has already been filled with meat. Forcing and dragging them from the road to the dark brush like the fragile quarry they are – and hacking them to pieces – is a simple style effort. The wolf's brain processes bright signals and data to obey. Its mindstate is a vague pleasure in orange light, while smells set priorities about the things to do. Under the full moon, a solid store of knowledge drives a desire of mass destruction. A sort of compulsive drug addiction that fuels rage with rage, in a blurry bloodshed. Food equals eating; human quarry equals killing. The whole human race must die, men and women victims of faults not their own. The wolf doesn't waste anything. It grabs, slashes; it slits and eviscerates from the open pockets with its claws, all the ruby-red bulbs of the organs it smashes in its fingers. The wolf snaps at trapezium muscles and rips with its teeth everything attached to the bones. Then the beast spits it off, if it doesn't want to eat. The wolf's blood is infected. It contains a peculiar virus genome transmitted by its saliva, which enters the victims' wounds and settles in their blood flow, despite current hemorrhages.

To kill. It wants to kill. It's a drug. The more it takes, the more it wants to take. Killing partly calms its hunger, partly the burning in its brain. That orange irradiation that grows and expands in the abyss of the mind – pushing it to run, smell, seek, hunt, kill, eat, run, and hide – wait for the night to raise its curtains for a new day.

Dead on the ground, a young girl. Her eyes no longer shine. They're lifeless, and dull, as though made of plastic, like a doll's. Death has changed so much about the once-alive harmony of features – the girl just a toy, now, created by a craftsman of little skill.

The wolf has virtually made her burst with its raging blows, so fast and so deep that her flesh still clusters in shiny crescents under its nails. The wolf's rage is a bodily instrument, working more or less fiercely in accordance with the toughness of the human section to be broken or uprooted. Dismembering a body isn't easy at all. The wolf likes women, indeed. It enjoys slaughtering them, ravaging their tender, greasy sides, licking and marring their inner thighs – where it always finds traces of blood and urine, even the smallest. The prostitutes along the road piss without cleaning up afterward, the uric odor a full-blast call for the wolf, who loves to maul those filthy parts, sometimes still warm from periods.

But it hasn't much time. It must act quickly.

It's necessary to do it all on the grass, among the trees, where it is possible to run free, where nobody can see. It also needs a watercourse to quench its thirst, and wash the quarry's blood away. To leave no trace, to forget, to run away from the shadow that always pursues, disturbs, the woman that obsesses and controls it, jealous of its work, greedy of breaking every tie with that cursed disease spreading through its bites.

Then, going back home and waiting for daylight after the hunting trip.

Going to the bathroom looking for water.

Waiting.

For its breath to calm, for bones to shift, and muscles to stop their tremble and shake; for that orange bright light to turn off in its mind and disappear below the horizon of awareness.

Waiting for its heart to slow, to be quiet, relieved from every fear and anger.

Watching the world changing.

Behind the closed roller shutter of a window.

SOMEWHERE ELSE, SAME NIGHT

A White Russian at Adrienne's. Actually, this is not Adrienne's house, but her friend's, a rich architect on holiday. So Adrienne can stay here – on the Aventino hill – and do whatever she wants: chill out, have parties, host friends, and even use his credit card. Kitsch furniture, leopard and bear furs on the floor, columns, tapestries, china wares, peach-colored marbles. Total suck. But Adrienne is a Norwegian watercolor version of a seventies' Cybill Shepherd, but with longer blonde hair. Dark Mary met her at the Gay Village, where she had booked a couple of deejay-set nights – a great contract, big money for the closing dates. She had already seen the Norwegian giantess at Goa's, the night of Asia Argento's party. The stranger, in all her light, had told her, "I've fallen in love with you, my obsidian!"

Martyna's absence is becoming heavier. For either new opportunities or the bulky emptiness with which it fills her life – night and day. Mary wants to put herself to the test with that six-foot-five blonde. Mary wants to see what happens if she's able to make love with her, a perfect stranger; or if, instead, there's still something bonding her to Martyna.

She can't believe she's single, now, free to manage her own person in full independence. Under Martyna's pressure, Mary's awareness was painstakingly lit, her mind in over-vigilance, her eyes scanning every detail of the world. Since she's alone, a wind of recklessness is making her euphoric, and is in need of redemption. David's dead, and he hasn't left the world peacefully. And she's so absent-minded that a Deltapol private security guard on patrol has seen her getting out of her Polo, park behind Adrienne's car along San Giosafat Street, and enter the home. Such a pair of asses cannot go unnoticed.

Adrienne's apartment is awful, but the Persian carpet in red, black and golden Damask is the perfect stage for the show to begin. Just a short preamble: nothing to explain nor wait because everything's clear already, no formality at all.

The Norwegian is about to fly back home, her trip over, and nothing is more exciting than a terminal love born to explode and implode with the coldness of a small star. Northern people don't live under the typical guilt of Mediterranean folklore. It will be wonderful for Dark Mary to euthanatize that embryonic passion with inglorious, liturgical surgery.

The two L girls attack each other with ferocity after draining their White Russians on the blue Frau leather couch. Mary's slender body slams against the horny Nordic battleship. Her arm joints and ribcage creak loud as Adrienne's embrace wraps her with boa constrictor strength. Adrienne does justice to David's coils, which Mary no longer has. She cries a silent tear of joy and compassion. For a second, she wishes to die among those arms of lust.

The giantess holds the dark girl tight, making Mary plunge into her gorgeous breasts. The deejay is a miniature that whispers and moans into the mouth of the burning woman.

Mary undresses Adrienne, rolling on the carpet. She does so with suffocating slowness, postponing more hardcore endeavors to a quieter moment, especially waiting for the background music to stop. Adrienne thought Mary could be ignorant about her beloved A-ha. This moment of patriotic cult will last only minutes. Mary cannot have sex with that shit hanging in the air. Stuff for spotty teenagers.

She tries to kill that damn OST with slow petting, holding off the Norwegian, who seems to be burning with fever. The big one wants to overwork the small one in a storm of sighs, pleasures spasms, shivers. She's in a hurry of seeing Mary naked, to stick her into her mouth whole.

Mary stops her, trying to finish undressing the blonde. "Take On Me" is on its last chorus. Adrienne likes it so much. She loves to be led by slender Mary. She breathes her sweet, dry aroma of flowers and something she cannot recognize. Myrrh, maybe, or some sort of salty resin. The crotch of Adrienne's snug blue pants is moist and hot with her vagina's good mood. Mary guesses she could stick her arm in up to the elbow.

Adrienne naked is a mystic vision: a giant light-pink-skinned doll, platinum blonde hair, real 40DD boobs. Lowering the boiling Nordic's panties, a wire of drool stretches between her labia majora and the liner of the material. Adrienne is completely melted. She has a dead-fish stench, but Mary doesn't mind and goes on. Mary is going to dominate, so she grabs the woman's blonde head and pulls it between her thighs as she lays on her back against the carpet. That's where she needs a mouth.

Half an hour has gone by, and the A-ha death-rattles are already a bad memory. The record player is mute, now. Mary lifts the blonde's head and guides her infinite body over her own. She kisses her mouth, then lies down again. She opens her shirt, offering her skin to Adrienne's kisses, who licks and kisses her neck, her chest, her cold skin.

Mary lowers her own jeans down to her knees, revealing panties in black lace. Adrienne rises on her knees and finishes undressing her. She takes a look at Mary's tiny ankles, then her feet. She adores them. Slim and long and smooth-fingered, with well-carved phalanxes – those of a Greek statue. Her large tongue slides on Mary's fingers, the insteps on her soles giving Mary a series of shocks, again and again. The giantess swallows Mary's entire foot in her deep throat, a real saliva bath, washing it over with love and spinning tongue. With the other foot, Mary caresses the living tower, touching her soft breasts, pressing her toes between those two meat-pillows, then going down to brush that sweating open pussy, soaking it up to the ankle. Mary tries to penetrate her with her big toe while Adrienne licks Mary's calf and then bites the tender back of her knee. She recoils, then leans into her inner thigh, quickly falling into the open leather door of Mary's soul.

The Nordic licks and sucks everything. She paints all she can with her drool and her crazy rough tongue. She licks vagina, lips, taint, until breaking through her anus. She brings up Mary's pelvis, doing a fierce rimming like nobody's ever done before. The Viking knows well how to lick, kiss, and tickle the right spots; she owns a damn tentacle inside her mouth. Mary's nipples are piercing her skin; they could bleed out of sheer excitement. Adrienne is nearly tearing her outer lips, sucking like a vacuum. Mary's pleasure grows as Adrienne commands even more pain.

The dark deejay shouts her orgasms, coming again and again. A torrent is born inside her and runs throughout her body, blurring her sight. Mary squirts, covering the blonde's face in juicy fluid.

She's not missing Martyna at all. And whenever Dark Mary is not home, Yèlen ceases to exist. Why *should* she go back? Mary's not wearing her steel nails, now, but her thighs know no limits.

Adrienne drinks and licks the fluid on her face, amazed and shocked by her little skinny lover's intensity of pleasure.

The time has come.

Dark Mary closes her legs tightly, like a vice, catching the blonde's head on her pubis. A few seconds and the Norwegian coughs, drowning under another squirting jet. Mary squeezes tighter.

And squeezes.

The Viking tries to wiggle out of her clutch, mumbling words in Mary's vagina.

Mary squeezes even stronger.

Adrienne's head bursts. A dull racket of bones first, then a stream of blood and brain, a warm pink runny flood, all over Dark Mary's milky white belly.

"Oh."

SECOND NIGHT OF FULL MOON, MARTIGNANO LAKE, AUGUST THE 1ST

Alfredo saw what happened to the *man* arrested at the ghost industrial city. The RIS is analyzing the audiovisual report of his sleep. Once isolated in a secure room at the Celio Army Hospital – under sedatives, and tied to the bed – they took infrared and X-ray scans of Piotr, from head to toe; and EKG, EEG, CAT-scan and blood test. At dawn, that aberration woke up with his human features. He did not look like a Bull Terrier, or a baboon.

That Lombrosian freak is back to his original face.

The Marshal knows that the man is the fourth Russian from the slaughtered group of the racetrack Renault 5. He's under medical interrogation, now, conducted not by Fildor, but by an Army Lieutenant Colonel. Tied and intubated for instant sedation, he tells everything as his blood is analyzed at molecular level by the RIS, the polyclinic technicians, and the Army. At this point, they have all the ingredients to make the *Scanners* case a Roswell-like event. A State secret compelling all forces involved to a code of top confidentiality, putting on the table every possible measure, contract and sanction, promotion and bribe. Full whitewash.

Why keep seeking the truth if it may never be told?

All those frozen bodies in the morgue will remain souvenir pics in his head, and perhaps unsolved cases for *Chi l'ha visto?* – the popular missing-persons TV show – to eventually become a bunch of faces nobody will remember. "Disappeared without leaving a trace."

So, before a friend disappears, too, Alfredo is at the gate of Fildor's summer residence. It's a two-level cottage, colonial style, near Martignano Lake, north of Rome. Fildor could have been murdered. Or he could have deserted the Carabinieri Corps with the serious risk of a leak. If the public knew about werewolves on the loose across Italy, it would be a mass disaster. Even if *Scanners* can never be newsworthy, at least the carnage will be stopped. They have the wolf now. Fildor cannot just drop out like that, provided he's still alive.

Alfredo doesn't push the door phone button, and won't call Fildor's numbers. The ring would enrage the two Dobermans already barking, both for the intolerable heat and his presence at the gate. He has to watch the cottage from a distance, moving around the place without being noticed. The dogs must calm down. It's 8:30 p.m., and the last train to Rome Trastevere is at 11:00. He hasn't much time, but he has a spyglass he bought for the occasion. He needs to establish a link with his friend Fildor. The pathologist has disappeared together with four bodies, while his colleagues discovered that Piotr could change his shape into some mutant dog and vice versa.

A nearby hilltop is a good overlook on Fildor's cottage. From there, Alfredo sees his Mercedes Benz out of the garage, three quarters of the courtyard, and the two Dobermans trotting around nervously. The lights are on, so there's no doubt the pathologist's home. Logically, the Marshall should call for a squad. Even just for a ride back home. He must wait. From the hilltop, he cannot see enough. Alfredo is getting nervous. His pineal gland gnaws because something's wrong down there. He must climb down. No other birdwatching spots on the cottage. Better hurry and see what the fuck is going on.

After all, the wolf is under arrest now, under guard by the Italian Army.

Inside Fildor's house, Alfredo could find further bodies.

Back at the gate, he pushes the phone door button. The dogs start barking again like fools.

Nobody answers. Alfredo buzzes again. Peering through wall and gate, the Marshal can see a slice of the cottage. The dogs do their assault, scratching the iron door and growling and frothing. The man's smell drives them mad. By pure luck, Alfredo glimpses a window, and its roller shutter coming down. Fildor, or someone else, hopes the visitor will be driven away by the dogs. Alfredo is looking for the best spot to climb the wall and leap inside. There, at the corner, a mass of ivy seems strong enough to support his weight. Now he just needs to find a way to knock out the dogs. Alfredo works the safety of his pistol and begins climbing the ivy.

"First we go up."

That's already trespassing.

This may be the very worst crap of his career, but the pineal itch tells him something big is waiting for him. The dogs rush in along the wall and they're so eager to bite his balls off. He could shoot them, but Fildor wouldn't be too happy about that. The two Dobermans are strong and nimble, and they climb on the wall, lizard-like, clawing at the concrete. They almost manage to jump up to the man and snap at his hands and face. Alfredo sits on the edge, heart in his throat, legs swinging outside.

He needs to think.

Suddenly, a racking scream from the house.

"Fuck," Alfredo says, swallowing.

The dogs stop and run toward the cottage, one after another, heads down. The main door is closed, so they run around to the back of the building. They're barking *inside*.

They're in, now.

Silence.

Yelps.

Two gunshots.

Silence, again.

Alfredo jumps down, he sprains an ankle. Shaking his foot, he draws his pistol. Then tries to run toward the door. He takes cover beside the closed window. Behind which, someone screams. Three screaming voices. The dogs are silent. Certainly shot dead.

Fildor yells.

"Fil! Are you okay?" Alfredo cries at the window. "It's Alfredo. Who's there with you?"

"Go away." The pathologist is in the dining room beyond that window. He sounds like he's down on the floor, in pain.

"Let me in. If you're in danger, I'll call for backup."

"Don't even try. Fuck off, man."

Fildor shoots.

Two, three shots at the window. The Marshal realizes his mate is shooting *upward*. Perhaps he's wounded – surely out of his mind. Alfredo thinks he could provoke his friend into firing his last rounds.

"Okay, man. I won't call, but I'm coming in. I'm breaking in now. Is there anybody with you, man?"

Fildor shoots his fourth and fifth bullets. The last ones, if it was *him* shooting the dogs. The bullet holes in the roller shutter are random. His hand's tremble. Fildor is at the end of his tether.

"Mate, I only want to help. Open that fucking door or I'll smash it in."

"Go away, jerk, if you want to live."

Alfredo Vanacura sidesteps toward the front door and opens it, shooting at the key-lock.

Then, he goes in.

Fildor is lying on the carpet of the dining room. He's lethally wounded, slashed open as though he'd fought that wolf-man. He's lost a ton of blood. He wheezes as he drags himself across the carpet. He raises his gun and aims it at the Marshal, then the weapon drops from his trembling hand. Fildor collapses on the floor, exhausted.

Alfredo hurries closer, takes him in his arms. He lifts Fildor's head, urging him to spit the blood filling his mouth.

"Who did this to you, mate?" he asks, close to tears. Then, he hears noises from the other rooms.

"Don't worry about it. They're chained," Fildor says, gurgling blood. A black thread spills from the corner of his mouth.

"Chained? Who the hell –"

The pathologist laughs. "I bet you know that already. But you're the same old insecure … you need confirmation."

Fildor's face is cut through by a fierce scratch. He's naked, except for trunks. Blood is splattered all over his chest. It seems someone has clutched his left arm, lacerating his brachial artery, as Fildor was trying to fight. The Marshal takes off his soaked shirt and knots it under Fildor's shoulder to try and stop the bleeding. "C'mon. Tell me what the fuck is going on."

Fildor is pale like a wax candle, but he still has energy left to talk. "I swear, my friend. I'm not crazy. It's not like my job fucked up my mind," the pathologist says.

"Why shoot at me, then?"

"To protect you."

"Protect me? From what? It's *you* shooting at me."

"You … you've got to listen to me, Alfredo."

"Talk to me. I'm listening – but I'm calling the ambulance."

"Think hard about who you're calling. In here, we've got four werewolves. Do you believe in werewolves, Marshal?"

"Oh, no. Of course not," Alfredo lies. "Even though –"

"Better you go and see them. Those four bodies from the racetrack."

"I know. The ones that disappeared from the morgue, Fil."

"Let me finish."

"Sorry, mate."

"Those four fucking bodies were lying on the autopsy tables of my lab, Alfredo. About six in the afternoon, same day we found them, and one woke up. And it could not – sorry – should not be alive. Same for the others. His two Russian friends and the slaughtered girl, too, reanimated one by one. Slowly."

"What the hell are you talking about?"

"They gradually awakened. Clinically dead, their main organs shut down, but they all began to wake up."

Alfredo wipes the sweat around his mouth with the back of his hand.

Noises from the other rooms.

Goddamn, who's there?

"The same wounds, the same killing hand. The ones we found with their heads exploded had woken just like those I had in front of my eyes. Someone had drilled their skulls to make them die."

"But why?"

"They say that Doberman dogs' skulls stop growing before their brains do, so they go mad. I keep thinking about this tall tale since the day we isolated the killer's mutant chromosome."

"For God's sake!" Alfredo says in a daze. In a second, in his mind a supernatural texture appears, which suddenly vanishes in a cloud of ideas.

"I was going to faint, seeing those bodies bend and sit on the table, and looking around like they were lost. But it was my opportunity to monitor the killer's victims. I injected myself a light dope and I began thinking steady. I had time to immobilize them to the tables. I inspected them and took pictures. I wrote everything down. Then, I took them here."

"What did you have in mind?"

"My silver pen could've been useful, but I'd lost it that night at the *Obituary*, do you remember? So I killed one of them with a dose of silver nitrate. Then, I figured out the biological cycle of these poor fellows. I took the second Russian and drilled his skull before his shape-shift. His head exploded just yesterday night, as he was turning from man into something else."

"So, what are they? Why do they change? How can it be?"

"Oh, shit," Fildor says, coughing up blood. "Alfredo, they are wolves. Werewolves. Or something turned them so. Some virus. The first sample of blood we took changed itself from man's to dog's, according to precise phases – once a month, for three days. This DNA is variable, able to alter that of healthy people it comes into contact with. It causes a sort of rabies and *canine transitory acromegaly*. If you don't have silver to kill'em, you need to shoot them in the head." He pauses. "Aim here," Fildor says, touching Alfredo's forehead with his fingertip, just on his third eye. "And *bang*."

"Tell me what you wanted to do with these corpses in here ..."

"They're not dead. And I didn't *want* to, I *had* to."

He's going to die.

Alfredo calls Captain Salvatores.

"What? *What* did you have to do?" Alfredo says, crying a tear as the Captain answers.

"Wait for a full moon."

Alfredo is in the bedroom now.

From the window, he can see the full moon above the clear sky, which makes him think about Piotr.

So, maybe the man-wolf who slashed young people at music events had accessories?

Alfredo faces the girl slaughtered at the racetrack – that thing *has to* be Valentina. He remembers her features exactly, but now her face is completely distorted, transformed. Now, she looks like Piotr, apprehended only twenty-four hours ago, with his altered dog features, only to awaken at the Military Hospital with human appearance.

Who's whose wolf?

And what to do with these creatures deported by Fildor at his home? It doesn't make sense. They can't be Piotr's accessories. They are victims, and that makes Piotr a victim, too, not the killer. Victims of someone else.

Another wolf?

They've changed shape after being attacked. And if someone had sabotaged their skulls, they'd have exploded at the first night of full moon during their metamorphosis. The girl's body no longer shows her wounds, maybe absorbed through the shape-shifting process. Some days before, that same girl was peeled off and gutted like a fish. If only she stood still, now, Alfredo could see the scars of her last day as a human being.

It's all so absurd. An anthropo-illogical madness.

But just looking at the she-wolf – who snarls at him, hissing and baring her dog-like teeth, gums withdrawn – is enough to realize there's no time to understand, or to believe, but only to see and act.

The she-wolf drools and sweats. Her wrists are getting sawed in the handcuffs secured to the bed. The blood she's losing slowly drips, as though not running through her veins.

If the no-longer-girl manages to break free, Alfredo realizes, she will tear apart the stupefied man staring at her.

Out in the corridor, the two dead Dobermans Fildor had shot.

Maybe they were going to attack the human wolves.

Who knows what could have happened if the lycanthrope had scratched and bit them ...

Leveling the pistol, the Marshal walks over the dead animals and follows the violent noise and cavernous sighs from the other rooms. Inside the guest room, one of the Russian guys is chained to the heater. He has one arm free, perhaps the one responsible for Fildor's death. His clawed hand splits the air with a whip-like whistle as Alfredo walks in. His rage makes him pull and yank at the chain, crumbling the wall where the heater tubes are embedded. He swings his hand seemingly a thousand times.

Impossible to say how long the wall will hold.

The wolves snarl; they need to kill everything that moves.

They're awful, their features annihilating. Their glance is mortifying, depressing; those eyes disorient, and freeze Alfredo's blood. For a human prey, standing in front of them is an inevitable, sad, cruel death sentence. Alfredo has no doubt that Fildor's theory is more credible than it had sounded. There are other wolves roaming free, in search of blood and water sources.

Tonight?

Rome should be overflown by several helicopters. The Prefect would tell him to go to hell if Alfredo only dared ask for a stunt like that.

Alfredo opens the door and enters the living room.

One of the Russians lies on a table, his body in human shape. And not tied.

Must be the one killed with silver nitrate.

The fourth and last body lies on the floor of the fireplace room, sitting with its back to the wall. Its feet and hands tied with thick electrical tape. Head recently exploded. The brain matter on the floor glints, fresh and still warm. Alfredo keeps clear from the corpse. The burst has painted the wall a peacock wheel of red meat; and staring at it, Alfredo can see where the brain sods slid down all around the motionless dead.

That is the place where the last Russian waited for death. This is the second night of a full moon, so that man died about twenty-four hours ago as he turned from man to wolf.

The smell will soon become unbearable. There are already flies.

A single question works the Marshal's mind, like a crowbar at a door.

Where's fear now? I feel nothing.

Alfredo calls the Captain again to ask where they are. The Russian chained to the heater is literally dismantling the wall. Dull thuds reach Alfredo's ears like the ticking of a time-bomb. The Marshal doesn't want to shoot that man, that thing, in the head. The incoming squad is bringing tranquilizer guns. They will take the wolves away and intern them in the Military Hospital. End of story. So long as they hurry, Alfredo may get back to Rome in time to have dinner with his mother, Assunta.

Father Sebastiano is holding a new heart in his tired hands.

He's just finished drinking the astral juice of its existence.

He's hungry for a new soul. He must eat another; otherwise, that cardiac work won't be carried out with sufficient strength.

He found the new heart in his church. Still beating, dripping vital fluid; still carrying the warmth of the body it used to power. The muscle is nervously tense, small twitches to continue its meaty clockwork with foolish linearity. Reading the last minutes of its life, Sebastiano realizes the heart has been ripped out after an amazing moment of passion. That life died on the shore of a sea of love. The last image imprinted, through its old owner, stuns the pale priest's mind.

Sebastiano is shocked, confused. Excited, thrilled.
Long time since he had last seen a cunt.
"At last, I found you."

NIGHT OF THE LOVING DEAD, 2ND OF AUGUST

Last night of full moon.
Mary meets Martyna again, for the first time since David passed away. At home. Martyna was waiting for her in the dining room, sitting on a chair, with Peter Hammill's *Black Box* album playing – paused and restarted, paused and restarted – as though it were a broken record.
"You've got some nerve, showing up here," Mary says.
"Only to tell you I'm leaving you."
"Martyna, it's *me* leaving *you.*"
Martyna wears a white linen suit, wide shirt and pants, and wooden sandals at her bare feet. Her hair is a black cascade over her breasts, with no bra under the thin fabric.
"Where have you been? I've been waiting for you, since last night … You smell of blood," Martyna mutters, grinning and showing teeth. She sniffs the air. Dark Mary shifts as she walks by close to her. The D in *blood* sounding so exciting. The natural gap between her upper incisors always made lovely sounds whenever Martyna talked.
"After what you did, you don't deserve to know what I do."
"Oh, Mary. Please, don't tell me you're still whimpering over that fucking snake … I screwed him, okay? But he bit me inside, okay? What the fuck was I supposed to do? Maybe go around with that thing swinging from my cunt? Did you want me to use it like a dick? So, I am sorry. I apologize for that creepy shit, but I was forced to kill him and pull him out of me."
"I want to hear nothing more. I was out all night and then I took a walk around the city. Rested a while on the Tiber Isle. Just needed to see some colored lights close to running water."
"All alone?"
"Alone. Just like I am now. As you see, don't you?"

Martyna presses on. "Met anyone? How's your life without me? Are you screwing any brand new cunt?" She's getting upset again.

"How can you ask about my life? Your questions sometimes, no, never ... they *never* make sense."

"Don't you dare," Martyna insists. "You can't just dismiss me like that." She rises and limps toward Mary, standing in front of her. The slender girl turns her back and enters the bathroom. Martyna follows and moans, "I want to know if you met someone."

"I've beaten you. I've kicked you out of my house. You came back, yet your bones haven't even healed. How many orgies do you think I've been in ... in less than a week? Time runs faster than real life in your never-ending paranoia. Of course, yes, I've just met a *lot* of people on the Tiber Isle. Still full of people. It's summertime, you know. And this is Rome."

"Rome. Rome. I hate this fucking Rome." Martyna's bones creak with rage. The noise of her fire.

"Go back to New York. Move. You can go anywhere in the world. Grab a fake passport and fly wherever you want. Just like I always did, until I ran into the dead-end of *your* sick existence."

"You little whore. You're not going anywhere," Martyna says, melting with rage. White foam at the corners of her full lips develop as her eyes fill with tears. "Tell me why you smell of blood."

"You know why. I've got a lot to do, here in Rome. You're the one who's supposed to go away. Or I'll behead you with teeth and nails."

"Please, go ahead. I prefer dying rather than living without you."

"Three advices, Martyna. Go back to New York City. Fall in love with someone closer to your needs. Get back working on your career as a photographer. Here, you're worth shit."

Dark Mary couldn't use a better poison. She's just spat mother Tamsen's favorite sentence of hate at her. Artfully humiliated.

"I need to follow my passion," Mary continues. "I can only be engaged to my music. You're a jail. You knew me as a deejay, and that's what I'll be, as long as I wish. I need it. And I can't be stopped, nor do I deserve being frustrated by you tormenting me. I belong to myself, first, then to my music, and to the crowd. I'm a message beyond time, a spirit, a feeling. You're pure paranoia."

Martina shuts her eyes, baring her teeth in a grin. Squeezed by her rage, her uterus is pouring – out of its still-healing wounds – a ruby-red oil.

Dark Mary notices the bloody iris spreading on her white pants. Martyna gets closer, hissing anger in Mary's face, but she doesn't step back. Martyna begins to undress, furiously, her breath short. Every move she makes, her joints rumble and resound, while her shaved vagina drools blood. Her skin quickly gets darker, white purple clouds that join one another. "Mary, you're just like that bastard, fake-straight, middle-class cocksucker that was my mother," she says, snickering. The veins of her neck swell, pulsate, covered in sweat, tendons pulled in over-tension.

"That's why you love me, I guess," Mary whispers, getting naked, too. The dark deejay stares at Martyna's eyes – silver discs ready to lose themselves below a tangle of thin capillaries. "I'm nothing special, Martyna. I'm only a model, a homeopathic replica for your psycho flaws."

"Enough with your bullshit," Martyna growls. "I love you. That's all, damn slut."

A lazy red steam rises from Martyna's shoulders. Blood evaporating on her naked skin. The smoke of her fury. The necrophotographer embraces Mary, arms around her waist. She clings to her as though meaning to break her in two.

"Accept me for who I am, Martyna. An alter ego your sick mind has chosen for you. Once you understand this, you'll let me go. We'll let each other go, toward better destinations."

Dark Mary caresses Martyna's naked shape. No doubt, in her mind's eye, the vastness of Adrienne's flesh still lives in a colony of dramatic torment. Martyna, though, is special her own way – for better or worse. And she's sadly irreplaceable.

The head of the raging woman rattles from chin to nape. Her face is pulled by hundreds of invisible hooks as her skull trembles under her skin, like a surface of water under heavy rain. Her whole body shakes in spasm, all her joints and cartilage sounding like a landslide of pebbles.

Dark Mary brushes Martyna's breasts, warped by concentric

waves spawned by an energy blindly running through her body. The red steam rising from the blaze of the woman's majestic rage vanishes against the ceiling, leaving a light brown mark. Martyna wishes to say something, but her distorted larynx can only articulate a barking turmoil. Her lips tear as her face wedges forward, her nose and mouth turning into a long snout, of great bite and deep smell. Fur proliferates, sizzling under a hurricane of hormones throughout her skin. Ears flex back, sharpen and bend, like ram horns.

"I love you, but not your heart." Dark Mary scratches Martyna's breastbone, already overcast by a quick crowd of stains. The cut gets deeper and deeper, until Mary's hands stiffen, and her steel French manicure breaks open her lover's chest.

Martyna growls in her face, lifting her shoulders.

DMj rummages inside Martyna's ribcage, holding her tight, kissing her full-wolf jaws. Mary breathes her boiling breath, washes herself in drool, and lets the monster tighten her grasp with arms of brutal fierceness, bestial muscles and claws.

Mary's scalpel-nails surround the wolf's heart. The organ beats like living wood, ever faster, as though about to explode. "I can rip it out, or cut it and weaken you. Enough to get the right weapon and kill you once and for all," Mary says. She applies a little pressure with her fingers, and the wolf is disoriented by a sudden whistle in its ears.

Martyna eases her grasp on Mary's waist, vaguely trapped by pain. It can't talk with canine vocal chords; the wolf can only listen to Mary, understand and accept. If little Mary wants to tear out its heart, then she will smash her head and that will be the true end. The wolf's body can take and heal any wound through the cycle of mutations, unless Mary uses silver or destroys its skull. Or maybe, she will only drill it, so the wolf will die in pain. Martyna tries to control her anger as Mary draws her hand out of its chest, leaving the wolf's heart intact. Martyna grumbles a bit of surrender. Then, standing still on her paws, lets Mary kiss its chest and stiff belly, which reveals six other flabby and milk-poor tits.

Mary tames the wolf, guiding it to the floor. Martyna keeps growling, with no intention of being subdued and offering its throat. Mary wishes to suck its dusky, furrowed tits, through the fur and sweat. Panting and lying on its side, the wolf is wary of offering the whole belly, even though its alert, thunderous senses receive no emotional emission from Dark Mary, who, now naked and wet, makes her assault on the wolf's tender flesh, the spread-open hind legs, and up to its sexual orifice, licking and nibbling it to soothe its impetus.

The wolf's whisper is a low whistle, almost ultrasonic.

But that's not a whistle of pleasure.

The wolf takes its pleasure from blood, from the stripping of flesh, from deboning, and mauling fat tissue and meat ripped from the sides of human quarry.

No. No.

No.

Martyna bends, suddenly. Its body arches in less than a second upon Mary, surprising the little deejay as she sucks the meaty bud formed by the mutated flaps of Martyna's vagina. Swinging its claws like sabers, the wolf lays waste on Mary's naked back, grooving and splintering its long nails against her ribs. The beast randomly rips Mary's flesh between thighs and butt, turning her loins into a squeezebox of sliced muscles. With immense strength, the wolf stands, grabbing little Mary by her neck and ankles, and throws her headfirst against the wall. The vertebrae in the deejay's neck crumble.

Mary slithers down the wall and collapses on the floor. Then, a storm of slashes reaches her, severing her skin into dozens of bloody stripes. Martyna's claws don't stop, with blows to her belly, to her helpless arms, her legs, until the wolf has finely ground every last portion of flesh, thorough, not to leave any pink spot across the pounded mass.

Until dawn.

Until the sweet, nervous and slender Dark Mary is a dummy of pulped meat.

Until from her head, shapeless and faceless, a tired tear slides down to meet daylight.

PART THREE
WASTING

Alfredo doesn't hang out on the World Wide Web. Stubbornly, the last analogic Marshal prefers print media. To work on his researches, though, he gladly takes advantage of the Carabinieri station in Bologna square, where he can breathe the rose scent of Miss Palmieri, the young Sergeant managing information technology. Moreover, the line 62 bus can leisurely take him there and back to the Jewish ghetto.

Palmieri is ready with Google Maps at her desk. Alfredo is ready, too, with a stack of music magazines to find matches. On the agenda he can't manage, he's written the dates of death for every wolf victim. Fildor never made mistakes in his autopsies. His reports about the first bodies were pretty detailed. Priscilla, Roberto, Alberto, and the four Renault victims: all had gone to a Dark Mary performance, attacked by the wolf either during or immediately after the show.

Coincidence?

On his agenda, Alfredo noted the name of each club and their addresses, but as soon as the Marshal realizes how fast Sergeant Palmieri is at her PC, he flushes and puts away the bundle of magazines.

Useless.

Acknowledging defeat in a gentlemanly manner, he works with her, highlighting possible escape routes of the victims, from DJ set to place of death. The hunted is chased by the hunter, and their passage may have been grabbed by security cams – banks, private houses, shops.

"We still have to understand," Alfredo says, thinking out loud, "if the killer acts alone, or if there's some kind of master behind the wolf, or someone who follows and then drills ..."

The young Sergeant isn't in the loop about *Scanners*. Alfredo didn't bother to ask Salvatores for clearance. Waking up from his mental process, he realizes the Sergeant has perfectly good ears and that he's already said too much, so he stops mid-sentence.

Palmieri frowns, but she's smart enough to erase embarrassment with a saucy, "Marshal, if you're trying to entice me with your suspense storyteller skill, I have to remind you of my wedding date: September, the 20th."

"Oh, sorry, but ..." Alfredo says, without finishing his sentence. "Sure, I would be happy to receive the announcement card. I would be glad to attend. If I survive this infernal summer." Maybe he'd better stitch his mouth.

"Really too hot, this year, Marshal," the Sergeant agrees. "A glass of ice tea? You look so tired. Are you okay?"

Palmieri is so cute and charming. And gentle.

"Thank you. I'm fine. We must locate security cams all along this route here, and get all footage since early March."

Alfredo sits beside her. His request is pretty weighty.

Palmieri's blood rushes to her face, but of course she can't say no.

"Well. Let's start."

Her lovely fragrance causes the Marshal to feel the sting of a lack of a woman's companionship in his life. Besides his mother, Assunta, of course.

"Do you know anything about this Dark Mary, Sergeant?"

Palmieri smiles, staring at the computer monitor. "Affirmative. Who doesn't? She's a really famous deejay. I've been at her shows many times." Then, the woman takes a look at the Marshal's eyes. "Gone with my fiancé. He's *very* jealous. Woe to anyone who gets too close to me. He comes everywhere I go. Even when I'm on patrol, in uniform, he watches me from a distance. I know it sounds –"

"Yes, of course!" the Marshal yells.

Palmieri startles.

Alfredo's face is alit. He watches her as though he'd like to kiss her.

Another rush of blood to her cheeks.

"Are you really okay, sir?" she asks, worried.

"The lover goes everywhere the loved one goes."

"Let's start breaking down the character myth," says Radio Rock DJ Armandino, live from their studios, after welcoming his listeners. "Who's really Dark Mary?"

"Dark Mary DMj is a meta-dead," Mary says, approaching the mic with her mouth in whispered revelation. "Namely, a person who lives, although she's clinically dead."

Very few of her fans ever heard her voice before. And never on the radio. This is a big event.

DJ Armandino opens his eyes wide, and hints at a smile. "I guess this claim will get us flooded in emails. So, Mary, what do you really mean by saying you're a *meta-dead.* Maybe you –"

"During a coma," Mary says, cutting him short, "regular brain functions are suspended, together with awareness. Meta-death is the opposite: the body is dead, but the brain is vigilant, and manages the whole person. Her existence, her biology. A meta-dead behaves like someone who's alive and healthy."

"Do you want to play a particular song to undersign this very first profile of Dark Mary?"

"I'd say 'Some Chords' by Deadmau5's," Mary answers.

"Pay attention, friends. The queen of metal rock has a love affair with house music."

Dark Mary's black-painted lips smile. "Music has no borders. It's the land where all citizens communicate using the same language."

DJ Armandino starts the song and, with the music in background, begins reading emails sent by listeners. "Emanuel says: 'I am drawing, fast and furious, a bunch of comic pages for Marvel, and I'm late on my deadline, but I had to stop and listen to this. Mary, tell us everything about you.' Betty says: 'Bloody kisses to the real queen of today's rock.' Eugenio says: 'I saw you at Radio Rock Beach. You're the greatest. Please don't stop.' And Alessandra says: 'Dark Mary, our angel, give us records until the Day of Judgement.'"

Mary listens. Then she speaks: "Thank you, thank you all. Really, from the deep of my heart."

"Dark Mary deejay, here with us, from our sweaty Radio Rock studios, 106.6. It's 4:33, live-streaming on *radio rock roma dot com*," the speaker says in his steady, warm voice. "So, Mary. I can say that this is the very first time your audience can hear your voice. And that I'm leaving you all the space and time you wish. What's the secret of your charisma? Why did you choose a gothic dark look?"

"That's not a matter of choice. It's not a *look* at all. I'm just the one you see. I'm a *nomen*, a meta-dead. The beating of my heart, as well as my breath, is commanded by will. Because my body is dead."

"Wait. Wait. Wait. What does *nomen* mean?"

"It means *name*, in Latin. In English, 'no-men,' as in *inhuman*."

"You really are a living legend. How did this all begin, Mary?"

"It began around the end of the eighteenth century, in Vienna. Mother Yèlen inherited this aberrant life condition from her father, Jacob. My grandfather worked as a butler for a German surgeon, Rudolph Werner. This man was devoted to esoteric rituals; among others, a strange worship of coffins. He owned one made in Transylvania, where he used to sleep at night. One night, while the old surgeon was working at the hospital, Grandfather Jacob decided to secretly enter his master's coffin, to try and comprehend such a chilling habit. He fell asleep, and when he awakened he was completely changed."

Dark Mary reveals her genealogy as briefly as she can.

"Via sex, Jacob infects my grandmother. My mother inherits meta-death, and contaminates my father, Conan, always via sex. I got it at conception. My father escaped when it was no longer possible to hide my family disease. Perhaps he long since found a way to kill her parents and himself, after trying to eliminate me and my mother."

"Sorry, Mary," the speaker says, keeping an eye on the computer monitor. "We've got an email from someone named Monica. DJ Armandino reads it elegantly, no judgement, no emotional involvement: 'Exciting story. Dark Mary, you made us dance. It's been a year that you've gotten our trust and our wallets. Now you're telling us you're two hundred years old? Please, not another fucking Marilyn Manson. You're great, but it seems success has gone to your head. Give up the bullshit or you're losing many fans. Be yourself."

"I'm aware that my words can puzzle you, Monica," Mary says. "I respect you. I'm thinking about my Mary Army. I want to arrange meetings, and mass listening, not for parties or to make money, but to discover new musical territories together. I won't ask you to believe me. Just follow me, and only if you want to. I'm here to spread music. The ticket prices for my shows are set by festivals and clubs that host me. I have no say in it. Besides my honest fee."

"We want to believe you, Mary," DJ Armandino says. "You're the best deejay in Rome, and maybe in all Italy. I'm saying this, as any other true deejay should. So, choose another song and then a quick commercial break. Then back to you. How does that sound?"

"Okay. Well, I'd play Hole's 'Nobody's Daughter' because, just like me, many of us feel this way. Male and female alike."

After the break, Dark Mary doesn't wait for further questions.

"The nomen see their backs in mirrors. That's why I need someone to help me with my makeup and outfit. Someone with a lot of patience."

"Tell us more about the nomen, what do they do?"

"The nomen feed on human flesh and blood. It's the only way to keep their bodies from rotting. The meta-dead lives the anguish of existence at its fullest, with dramatic devotion to the human race, and not only as a means for survival. Usually, nomen pursue fine arts and knowledge. I chose music, and here I am today."

"Are you really saying that you kill to stay alive? This is some strong contradiction with the love you show to your fans."

"I know. Mine are not wanton killings. The Jewish community I belong to knows persecution well, since time immemorial.
Those who die for me don't fear death. I kill to spread my message to the world. I steal the hearts of the people I feed on, and hide those hearts in God's house, so that the light of Christ can destroy the shadows in which they would otherwise lose themselves."

"So, what's your message?"

"I've just told you. And I think it's really striking. I don't bring the hearts I rip out to a synagogue, but to a Catholic church."

"Folks, the voice you're hearing right now is Dark Mary, here in the flesh. This year's most loved deejay, a Radio Rock discovery, a rising star. Let's read the last email and say goodbye to Mary. 'Hi, Mary. My name's Andrea. I'm not into metal at all, but for me you're number one. I'd just like to know what happened to the white python.'"

Dark Mary begins to cry.

Alfredo and Sergeant Palmieri stay tuned to the words coming from the computer speakers. It's been the Marshal's brilliant idea: searching *Dark Mary* in Google. They were just in time for the streaming of the interview.

"Did you hear that, Marshal? Isn't she fun? Mary is a real rock star. A bit phony, but an extraordinary character."

"So extraordinary that I need to smoke a joint right now. I must meet her. Hurry, please, get me the address of the radio station."

Sergeant Palmieri quickly finds it, and she calls a car for the Marshal. He runs toward Radio Rock, hoping Mary's still there.

During the ride, Alfredo thinks about what to say to Mary. He's also considered the most obvious theory, therefore the first to discard: that Dark Mary herself is the killer. Of course, her words connect with the *dry maggots*, not the wolf victims; of course, wolf attacks happened even *during* her performance, so she has an alibi confirmed by thousands of people. It's a process of elimination.

Those magazines were good for something, after all.

Reading Dark Mary's name on paper, and matching with the dates of the killings, led him this way, making his pineal gland itch with a brand new level of intensity.

When it itches, I have to run, Alfredo thinks. *I never decide shit. Suppose the wolf attends Mary's performances; so we should find there, too, the one who drills the victims' heads, or rips those guys' hearts after bleeding them out … admitting it's really the same person. And why do I think so? Why did Mary say on the radio it was her?*

Her confession makes no sense.

And then: *Why should the wolf follow Mary?*

Not to mention that the victims were never abducted, nor buried.

The killer seems not to have time or strength to do it.

The killer must be a woman, he thinks. *A woman who goes to Dark Mary shows and has something to do with the wolf. A fan? A weaker theory would be that she knows Dark Mary. A friend. And, of course, there's the big issue: How can Mary know about the bled out, heart-ripped people? She knows something, that's for sure. Maybe she's trying to say something, a stunning truth. Playing on the fact: Could anyone believe what some darkish deejay says on the radio? It's only rock and roll.*

"What the hell am I thinking?"

"I beg your pardon, sir?" the plainclothes driver says as they arrive to Radio Rock Studios. A thick crowd occupies the street. Alfedo couldn't foresee that; they're all Mary's fans.

"Sorry," Alfredo answers. "I was just thinking out loud. Well, thank you. I can get out here."

"Sure, Marshal. I'll wait for you here, sir."

Under the five o'clock sun, Alfredo reaches the front doors of the studio and pushes the door phone button. He had to wade through a multitude of metal teens both hairy and sweaty; he's the lonely over-50 in that bedlam. He tries to study those gazes, coming from eyes heavy in make-up, pale faces in typical rock concert getup.

Did they ever hear half a riff of "Sabbath Bloody Sabbath"?

His gaze mustn't be insistent, he tells himself, as the killer may not be one of those underweight children, notwithstanding decorative chains and studs.

Before leaving the fans and entering the radio building – he murmured the magic word *Carabinieri* to the security man watching over all the packed people on the street – Alfredo contrives a concept that cheers up his raid into the place.

Dark Mary used the truth to her own advantage.

His pineal itches.

The Marshal must wait in the reception of the most loved Roman radio station. The interview is still on-air. Nobody has anything to hide, but a Carabinieri Corps visit casts free question marks on everyone's face. Back in the seventies, twenty-year-old Alfredo Vanacura loved rock, too. He loved free radio and shared anarchist politics and ideals; he was a pacifist and anti-statist, while the whole world was going upside-down.

The station phone rings non-stop. Prince Faster, the elder deejay, explains to the Marshal that Mary guest-starring is a real, epic, mass-hysteria event.

"Why are you looking for her? Are you arresting her, asking for an autograph?"

"Nope. The girl's got talent and a lot of imagination. I think she's a great rock star. I'm only interested in meeting her. I didn't know how to."

"Then let me invite you to her next DJ set," Prince Faster says, "at Ostia, Radio Rock Beach."

"I'd love to, but I don't have a car."

"Call a taxi. Please, not a patrol car, though. Otherwise, our guest may worry a bit. We can offer you a lot of good drinks."

"Thank you, Prince, but I don't like cocktails," Alfredo replies.

"We have fruity soft drinks, and tonic water as well. No problem. Please, come, Marshal. That's a very quiet place, our beach. We only had a single accident in twenty years, and not even serious."

Prince leaves him as Mary appears, saying goodbye to DJ Armandino and other colleagues at the reception desk.

"Dark Mary?" Alfredo says. A cough. Why is he so embarrassed in front of a little girl?

"Yes. It's me." Pale, curved and slim like a cherry-wood branch, dressed in pitch black, black eyes, black hair. Ring at her nose, left nostril.

"Nice to meet you. My name's Alfredo. I'm a Carabinieri Marshal."

Dark Mary stares at him for a long moment. No expression on her face. Then, she walks on toward the main door.

"Excuse me," he tries again, following her. "Just a second," he says in a lower voice.

Dark Mary pushes the front doors and the crowd's scream floods her.

"Wait. There are hundreds out there." Alfredo reaches her shoulder, hoping to stop her. "Mary, one moment. Please."

Please? I could arrest her. She's a suspect, knows classified things.

"Tell me, Marshal."

And yet ...

The crowd rejoices. The security guards, well-trained for concerts and crazy night shows, contain the pressure of that pushing horde at the front door, where Mary just appeared.

"Why say those weird things on the radio?"

"Are you going to arrest me or not?"

"Oh, no. I'm an open-minded man. I only want to ask you why you talked about cannibalism and living dead. Sounded rather weird to me."

"Weird? That's my culture, my way of being. Does anybody ever point out to you how *weird* is being a Marshal?"

"I'd point out that cannibalism is an illegal practice, Mary, but aside from that, the matter here is your imagination. The things you said on the radio to thousands of people."

"I really don't understand why you're talking about fantasy. That's the biggest trouble with humans, Alfredo. We're in a never-ending fight to understand, to be understood, and to be accepted."

The Marshal is lost.

As she speaks, that girl makes his heart burn and his tongue tie up in his mouth. His brain is in a washing machine, now in bleaching mode.

C'mon, idiot, it's only a little girl.

"May I ..." Alfredo says, messing up his hair and biting his lip. An embarrassing pause. "May I come to your next show?"

"The correct phrase for my shows is *deejay set.* You can come whenever you want, Marshal. I certainly won't stop you. However, I suggest you to come."

Alfredo doesn't have the nerve to say, *I've just busted a bunch of werewolves and collected bodies, dead, just the way you mentioned them a few minutes ago.* Alfredo contents to watch her going out, facing the mass of her lovers. They scream in triumph as she steps through the front door.

"I wish I could talk to you, Mary," Alfredo says, as the girl is swallowed by the crowd shouting, "*Mary Mary, hey hey! Mary Mary, hey hey!*"

Mary turns for an instant and says, "Give me time."

"Yes, but –" he mutters. Two syllables, and the great Mary vanishes in the multitude.

Dark to dark.

"Do you know where she lives?" Alfredo asks the security guard.

"Sorry, I don't. Ask inside," the man grunts.

He's not a wolf, Alfredo thinks. *But a Rottweiler. He's okay.*

Alfredo goes back inside. In the main hall, he meets Prince Faster again and says, "Excuse me, Mr. Prince." A moment's doubt. "Can you tell me where Dark Mary lives? Or her real name?"

Prince shakes his head, looking at Alfredo without saying, *Marshal, please, don't ask the impossible.*

"Should I ask the producers?"

"Maybe. Maybe they can tell you more. To me, Mary is just an attraction contributing to the survival of my station."

"Thank you."

SPIDER WEBS AROUND THE PINEAL GLAND

At night, Alfredo is at the window of his flat, lost in thought. He's smoking his pipe under the few stars in the sky, staring up at the window of the attic of the building across from him.

That fucking closed window seems to constantly watch over me.

Dark Mary works for Radio Rock, so she must have a boss who pays her. There must be invoices, signed contracts with her real, full name, with her address, tax code, everything. He could have them quickly, if he wanted. He'd just have to call Captain Salvatores and go through official channels.

So, why am I not doing that? Pineal sparks, that's why.

She told the world she's a meta-dead, feeding on blood and human flesh. Her claims thus creating a direct connection to the bodies of those poor devils who went to her deejay sets. Logic would list her as an immediate suspect. But the timeline's not right, and it can't be so simple. And *Scanners* is top secret.

She practically confessed she's the killer.

Maybe Mary knows the real killer, and she appropriated cursed pedigree just to amaze the listeners, to boost her public image.

If I arrest her, maybe she won't say who the real killer is.

"That girl impressed you too much, old fool," Alfredo says to himself, blowing the sweet smoke out the window. "And this makes it all the more complicated. A real mess."

The Marshal goes back inside, grabs the cup of coffee he had prepared half an hour ago, forgotten on the desk until now. He takes a cold sip, swallows. Heartburn gas rises in his throat.

Back to the window, he burps against the fresh air.

"This is useless and it doesn't mean a thing. It's only a stupid coffee gone cold."

So, let's start again.

A cannibal assassin, with rabies and canine transitory acromegaly, devours girls and boys who go to Dark Mary shows.

Why?

Victims are killed a second time via skull drillings. Someone, maybe the wolf itself, wants to deactivate the plague it carries.

Why?

Other people are chased, bled, their hearts stolen. This ritual is then confessed on radio by the alleged killer herself. Yet *Scanners* is completely classified. Perhaps not even the Minister of Internal Affairs is informed about it. How could someone of his party ever comprehend something like that?

He'd sack us all, wholesale.

The only thing Alfredo can do is delve into Dark Mary.

His phone rings.

"Hello, Marshal, good evening," Sergeant Palmieri says. "I know it's late, I'm sorry, sir."

"No problem, Sergeant. Good evening."

"There's no relevant footage along those routes. No camera picked up anything out of the ordinary. I'm sorry."

"I'm sorry, too," Alfredo lies.

As you wanted: Dark Mary wouldn't show up anywhere.

"If I can do anything else, Marshal, please ask."

"Thank you, Sergeant. I'm sure you'll be helpful."

"Good night, sir."

Dark Mary is involved.

She knows something. Actually, everything.

"Pineal's talking straight."

Alfredo misses Fildor so much. His friend, his special pro. He shifts the books on the leather sofa, and lies down after taking off his shirt. Turning on a side, he can keep an eye on the attic window in front. Some minutes later, he stands, panting, his skin glued to the leather pillow. He turns off the light, lies down again, same position. In his mind, he tries to figure out a possible series of detailed studies and consultations. He'd need an astrophysicist to know about lunar influence, a parapsychologist to learn about neurological diseases like terianthropy, and then match all that to come up with a clear theory about aggressive cannibalistic fits, like those that made the Rostov Monster – and many others – notorious.

Alfredo looks at the front window, eyelids closing.

What the fuck is there, behind that closed win ...?

He falls asleep.

And dreams of Fildor, wearing a kitchen apron with blue and yellow flowers, cutting him alive on the morgue lab table.

Alfredo wakes up screaming.

The dream had replayed the last conversation with the pathologist in his Martignano cottage with the wolves, just before Fildor passed away in his arms.

To protect you, he'd said, then.

Wait for full moon, he'd said again in the dream.

SUSANNA'S VERY FIRST TIME

Elisabetta is dying at home after years of pain and suffering. She cannot speak because a car crash had paralyzed her with several brain injuries. Father Sebastiano gives her last rites. He was called by her relatives and the family doctor. In this house, the bedsore smell is quite strong. It's God's will. Life is smoke, and everything Sebastiano wants is to inhale.

Sebastiano must eat her soul. Sebastiano is a soul cannibal. He needs to feed on human spirit. It's his disease. Flesh is a bluff that rots even on the surface of a bed.

Elisabetta can finally shut herself and escape her bodily history that, since she was born until this moment, has crushed her inside the metal sheets of a car. She flows downward. It's a sweet, dynamic sensation, like going down a slide with her face into the wind, but never touching ground.

She's going down a red room, now. And tight. A sort of living container made of flesh and bone, muscle and organ. Elisabetta opens her eyes again and can see the lights of her house filtered through Sebastiano's flesh. Of him, she's hearing the voice, the breath, his heart beating. The priest has swallowed her in some way, but it's impossible to move and communicate with him. It's not a nightmare. Elisabetta hears the voices and the cries of her parents and relatives surrounding the priest; they're only shadows, now, moving across his transparent flesh.

Sebastiano's matter is like the rose window of a church, the glassy decoration of a huge cathedral. Before passing, Elisabetta thought she would discover the fatuous emptiness of death, its unfathomable abyss, demons hunting her down. Instead, she's bottled inside another body – passed through by the light and sound of the living – in a sight of dominant red.

The living mass of the priest wraps and fills her. At the same time, she penetrates him, lost among fibers and tissues, slipping along connective fluids and elusive knots, cartilage joints. Elisabetta no longer has a mind, so she must not think, and she's free from every fear because she isn't alive anymore and she doesn't have to struggle. Immersed in human matter, however, she's able to know who she is, and where she is, thanks to a weird inertial awareness rocked by his pushing breath. Now she knows she's a soul; what's left of a past existence. And this hot effluvium, coming from inside Sebastiano, condenses her in milky, semi-liquid state: white at first, then orange, then rust, and brown, until thickening her in black. Turning into clay at every heartbeat, as though *his* heart were kneading her. Elisabetta soon becomes a cold, dark clot around the priest's heart as he walks and coughs, disturbing his footfalls on the asphalt road in the street lights.

Molded in thick bolus, she drifts inside his bronchus through a small trachea opening, to be breathed into the blind bottom of his lungs, where she discovers a similar layer much older than herself.

Upon it, she dozes off, dominated by the choking organism.

Mirella hears new noises from the flat above.

She's wearing only a nightgown, her hair is full of curlers. But she can't help it; she can only turn her nose up to the ceiling and wonder, worrying about her beloved Sebastiano: so thin, so emaciated, always in a daze. To her, the pale priest is a silent and elusive son. She loves him deeply, like an overprotective mother, even when she's afraid of looking him in the eye. So, she grabs the keys to his house, and she goes out to climb the stairs.

She knows the priest had to give a poor girl the last rites in the other side of the city.

Maybe he came back early and something's wrong.

She reaches the door and knocks. Knocks again.

Why doesn't he come?

If Sebastiano were home, he'd open. Even if he were sleeping, Mirella could knock at his door at any hour. So she uses her keys. Three turns and the door opens. Mirella enters.

The apartment is dark, except for some small, red graveyard lamps.

At the end of the corridor, against the soft light of the dining room window, is a human shadow.

A woman.

"Oh. I'm sorry, Madam."

The woman doesn't speak, but stands still.

The curtains let in the night light, a graceful wall of electric blue.

Mirella can't tell if the woman is facing the curtains or the corridor, doesn't know if the stranger is looking at her from the dark room.

"Who are you?" she asks. "Who's there?"

Mirella rubs her eyes. For a second, her sight becomes less clear, but soon she has no doubt. There is a woman standing in the middle of the dining room. She isn't having hallucinations.

"Are you waiting for Sebastiano?"

Mirella doesn't move. Even though she owns that flat, she's embarrassed of finding an unknown guest inside. She waits there, still holding the door handle. She doesn't have the nerve to walk across the corridor to that person. She begins to be afraid.

"So, what are you doing here?"

The shape moves, walking toward Mirella without a sound.

The old lady feels a cold wind at her chest.

Perhaps she's barefoot.

The thought is unreasonably chilling.

Mirella tries to move aside, to go back to the landing and close the door – three turns of the key.

Fear grows ever more. That mute presence is going to smash her fragile heart. She doesn't want to die now, but her legs don't move. Her legs have turned into stiff wood. Mirella pisses herself as the silent shape gets closer.

The red graveyard lamps struggle. The electric light on the landing comes and goes. Goes and comes. Mirella melts in fear as the features of the silent guest become definite in the weak candlelight of the corridor. She can fitfully see that the woman – never saw her before – is sleeping, yet walking.

Her skin is black like coal.

But maybe this is only a suggestion, a trick of the low lights. Her dark, motionless face comes to light and disappears in the shadows, appearing and vanishing as the lights die off, as Mirella's teeth chatter and her voice softens to a sad whining.

Finally the black-skinned woman, dressed in her red checkered dress, opens her eyes in the dark.

Silence and darkness, the same thing.

Mirella falls to the landing floor.

Her mouth half closed.

Eyes open wide and dry.

Grabbed by her thin ankles.

Pulled inside Sebastiano's home.

But now nobody can hear or see.

The door closing softly.

Locked as Mirella is swallowed.

Silence is floating nothingness.

DARK MARY BLACK BEACH PARTY NIGHT: 6TH OF AUGUST

"Not Promised Tomorrow," Stuck Mojo. "Odissey," Kyuss. "Rain," Cult. "Live to Rock," Saxon. "Nirvana," Cult, the live version. "Deliverance," The Mission. "Marian," Sisters of Mercy. "Map of the Problematique," Muse. "Breathe," Prodigy. "Jesus Built My Hotrod," Ministry. "Hey Boy Hey Girl," Chemical Brothers. "Yin and Yang," Love and Rockets. "Sulfur," Slipknot. "Violet," Hole. "Hair of the Dogs," Bauhaus, and "Helpless" by Faith No More. This is the only the overture of a schizophrenic set for the last night of a summer with Radio Rock. Each song has its own rhythm. Fast, medium-fast, fast. The audience is confused, forced to stop and change its mind to match each different beat.

Mary is just giving an example of the mass listening she announced on radio. She makes people's focus swing over the emotive variants of the different songs; to enjoy the music for what it is, and capture its poetry, song by song, through the entirety of each melody. If they want to dance, they only have to follow the beat. Mood and lyrics descend to a lower level of spiritual perception. People who want to move and shake fast are stopped, deterred from this need to discharge stress, as they're invited, forced to listen. As though this were a classic, goddamn rock concert. That's why so many stop dancing, stand still and look around, then scatter to chat and drink, away from the DJ tower. Here they are, those who won't be in the Mary Army.

That's too bad. The Marshal should have had the opportunity of tasting the real, giant love of the mass of people summoned by the dee-cannibal-jay.

The last rock festival he'd been to was back in 1980, when Kiss and Iron Maiden made their first Italian date at Castel Sant'Angelo. He was thirty, and the collective emanations during that night were very varied, but all extremely intense, and magically generated in unison. First, a colossal brawl, cut off by the Maiden sonic assault; their music was a real trauma. And eventually, the rock and roll party with Kiss.

Today is different. Mass is the participatory union of people. Everybody brings their own disorder, a neurosis. But Alfredo has changed, too, in thirty years. He's disturbed by mass gatherings. They bother him, hurt him. The crowd makes him worry about the problem of bacterial propagation.

What kind of mental structure underlies these people? What do they think? What do they believe in? Do they even believe in something?

Ignorance is viral, as well as dirty hands, or indifference to any means of prevention.

How many worry about defending against germs, bacteriological invasions, viral mimesis inside our food, dishes, air, contact outside homes?

Stomach ulcers are caused by bacteria, oral transmission. Herpes, fungi, parasites that grab the cloth of pants, staphylococcus riding the hands of whoever touched sick people. And the virus can only evolve into the best freakish expression of life and death. Tragedy turns itself into comedy, and a living dead is none other than the charade of God's will. A zombie is His perfect disowned son.

The atmosphere of this night on the beach is pervaded by a sense of dispersion caused by Mary playing songs disconnected to one another. This is her first DJ set since Mary made the weird confession about her history on the radio. Her fans seem to be here with a certain detachment, uncertainty.

Alfredo sees all this, and it's apparent how lonely that girl is in her life. The feverish worship of the mass outside the radio station, that day, has already changed into something weaker. The mass was out on the street waiting for Mary, then, without knowing what she was saying at that moment.

Now, her on-air bullshit has surely reached everyone.

Strangely, Mary – at her console in the DJ tower – looks as though she wished to sabotage herself, a clear sadness depicted by her static stance.

"Mary, I've got a problem," Alfredo says, staring at her eyes when they meet after the show. He gives her a cold bottle of beer, then lifts his own for a toast. Mary doesn't.

"Well, Marshal. Tell me, but, please, hurry. I'm pretty tired, and people have not reacted to my music. That's why I must sneak away fast. I won't give anyone the idea I'm here looking for approval."

Dark Mary should be a politician.

Alfredo isn't surprised by the little girl's solidity. And it's the main trait of her bewitching him. Not a matter of sexuality, but emotional, a matter of teenage mess.

"I'm sorry, Mary. Maybe it was too loud."

"Nope. It was my tracklist's fault. People want to go wild, not to listen. Nobody wants to listen. Never, Marshal."

"On the contrary, I want to. I'm asking only a few minutes of your time. So, Mary – oh … may I call you by your real name?"

"With pleasure. My name's Dark Mary."

"I get it. Well, I have a problem, as I told you. I believe in everything you said on-air during the interview, the day we first met."

"*Met* is a big word. *What* have I said?"

"Mary, you said that in order to survive, you must feed on blood and human flesh."

"I must not sur-*vive*, Marshal."

Alfredo frowns, sweating.

"I must sur-*die*."

REVELATIONS

"I know what you mean, Mary."

"So what?"

"Well, my dear. A lot of people think you make up things to boost your public image, your character," the Marshal blurts out. "That's all good, by me. When I was young, I used to be a Led Zeppelin fan and, honestly, I didn't fucking care about all that Satanist bullshit."

"I'm not —"

"Please, listen to me," Alfredo says, stopping her. "I approve of the things you do and say to fuel your charisma. It's your role. I'm not here to blame you or to investigate."

"Tell me what you want. Third time I ask, and you still won't answer."

Shit. Calm down.

"Okay, of course. Please, forgive me. But do you mind moving somewhere quieter? Too many people here. I'd wish to talk freely. That's impossible here."

"Let's go to the cabanas, where it's lit."

Alfredo turn to look at the area Mary's pointing.

"Good for me," he agrees.

She wants to stay in the light. She wants to be seen, to be watched. There's someone here with her, someone who watches over her, who protects her, Alfredo thinks, paying attention not to look around. *Someone who protects her.*

Walking across the busy tables of the cocktail bar, where Alfredo and Mary had their beers, they move away from the crows. Someone looks at them, says hello to Mary, but she doesn't reply.

The Marshal and the deejay step on a sand path and then on the concrete platform where the cabanas are lined up.

"I was telling you," Alfredo says, swinging his Ceres bottle in a circle to define his argument, "that story about you killing and drinking human blood, and stealing the hearts of those you bled out."

A solemn pause.

"Yes."

"I think that's true." Alfredo has a sip of beer.

"Right. Because it's real, Marshal. And I see you're not shaken by it, at all. That's so much more curious, isn't it?"

"They ..." Alfredo says, then pauses to search for better words. He rubs his nape. "They call me in as an unofficial supervisor of crime cases that require a distinct sensibility for supernatural matters."

"Marshal, I'm not supernatural. Only natural. What I said, you heard by my own voice. I am in harmony with my vulnerability more than anybody could believe. My body is my history, nothing else." Mary grabs Alfredo's wrist, causing a pain his bones have never felt. "Did you ever feel such a vacuum of energy? Let me hold it a little more, and your bones will disintegrate like an eggshell in my fingers."

Alfredo frees his hand and takes a look at his wrist. He touches it, finding it very cold. Like fist-fucking a cosmic black hole.

"Mary, please, listen to me," Alfredo says, rubbing the frozen wrist. "I discovered ... better, I am *collecting* bodies of guys and girls, tourists and tramps with not a drop of blood in their veins, and their hearts pulled out from their chests as easily as wallets."

"I knew it was going to happen, sooner or later," Mary whispers, wetting her lips with the Ceres.

"Hi, Mary," two kids say, passing closely. In a shy voice, one adds, "Mighty."

"Thank you, guys," Mary says. "Did you like the set tonight?"

She cannot do without gathering praise.

"Unusual night. But you're an artist."

They said it all.

"Perhaps someone didn't do their criminal work properly," the Marshal interrupts. "Mary, if you can tell me who kills these kids, I'd be very grateful. Nobody can have such a macabre imagination, not even you. You know who the killer is."

"Yes, Marshal. You could have asked an hour ago. *I'm* the killer."

"Oh, Jesus bloody Christ."

I must be going mad.

He tries to catch her smell in his nostrils, as much as he can, imagining it more intense and wild in the folded skin between her tits.

"Take a look, Marshal. Take a look at my nails. A friend of mine has made this French manicure for me." Mary fans her fingers in front of his eyes. "It looks like simple cosmetics, but each of these nails hides a steel backing that can cut through a wooden door. If you want to arrest me, do it, here I am. But we need to consider my physiology. You'll never be able to let go of me because I will persecute you, psychically, just like my mother still does with me, even though she's dead."

"Your mother?"

"You, Marshal ... could you ever manage a living-dead? What are you ready to sacrifice to share your short life with me? I will see you die, as well as all the other ones who'll come. You don't know what the dead who live can do."

"What are you talking about?"

"If you lock me in the cage of a jail, I won't eat anything but human flesh. Bowels, blood, muscles, bones, to be consumed by tearing and chewing on living people. You couldn't fool me with stuff from the butcher's. Would you and your colleagues give me someone to eat? Who'll be the one who give me my food, and who'll *be* my food? At what price? I'll survive any court, even any prison walls. And without the food I need, I will waste away, indefinitely, without ever dying. So my psyche will grip to yours, forever, until you die. I will infect you with sadness, depression, and dismay."

I'm getting lost inside Dark Mary's eyes.

He almost wants her nails to open his sweat-soaked shirt and her hand to stick inside his chest, clutching his heart and masturbating it on the spot, among all those people.

Mary keeps talking. "Besides the bodies you found, try and make a list of all the missing persons in Rome, in Italy, in Europe, and across the ex-USSR for the last two hundred years. I've been locked up for decades. I've been on the electric chair, hanged, poisoned, tortured, drowned, and burned. By luck, or misfortune, I missed out on the guillotine. Smashing my head is what it takes.

Nobody ever shot me in the head. You, or anyone else, would you do it for me?"

"No. I couldn't and I won't. But please, tell me who the killer is of the bled-out people. And, above all, tell me who drills the heads of the prey of that ..."

Alfredo can no longer bear Mary's gaze, so he turns to take a look at the crowd.

So after all, the one confessing isn't Mary ... it's me..

"Go on," Mary asks.

"... of that wolf."

"It's me killing those people, Marshal. I've got a French manicure made of steel, and a battery-powered drill. Do open my flight case, sir. You'll find it there, ready to use. It deters stalkers, but mainly it's necessary to stop the wolf plague. So, go on and seize it right now if you like."

"I won't, sorry. I've already stopped the plague. You can put away your drill in the junk room. We have arrested –" coughing, "– *captured* the wolf."

"That's fine. That damn thing was starting to annoy me. A real wearing-out relationship. We met in Helsinki, where we lived in hiding for years. Hunting country people, livestock thieves, and bastards."

"That Russian guy has infected a lot of people, but it's over now," Alfredo says. "The wolf is in isolation in a Military Hospital. We only have to wait for the next full moon, hoping there aren't any more wolves at large."

"I never miss one, sir. I can smell them, I sense the blood of their crimes from miles away, so I can get there and act in the right and final way. I'm doing this for the good of humanity. But now, please, enough. I have to go."

"We can go to my home. I have to learn more about you," Alfredo says.

Dark Mary heads off, leaving the Marshal behind on the concrete platform. Suddenly, she stops and turns back. She watches over the man's shoulder, then puts on her sunglasses, turns back again and resumes walking toward the exit.

Alfredo stays there, befuddled, until he has the strong feeling of someone smelling his nape.

He turns back.

"Marshal."

Alfredo has never seen a woman so beautiful: Adamantine light blue iris, slant-eyed, brown-skinned, nose and cheekbones quite African, full lips on snow-white teeth, plenty of space between upper front teeth. The Marshal is so thrilled by her perfect body that he can't hold his eyes from sliding down to the woman's breasts, and further, to see her legs.

"Do we know each other?" Alfredo asks.

"That could be an interesting chance."

Alfredo turns back once again, looking for Mary.

But she's vanished.

Then he turns toward the stranger.

But she's vanished, too.

This beer is too strong for me.

BLOODY NIGHT, THE LAST

Alfredo is aboard the station wagon Opel of Sergeant Palmieri and Giovanni, her fiancé riding back home from Ostia to Rome. A wonderful couple, beautiful and healthy. Giovanni isn't in the Carabinieri Corps; he's a library archivist.

Very kind guy, he thinks. *Right for the Sergeant.*

Alfredo sits in the back. He hates safety belts, which prevent him from enjoying the ride.

"I still don't know how to thank you," Alfredo says again, maybe for the third time.

"Marshal, I told you already. Whatever I can do, you must count on me. Not only when music's involved."

"By all means, Marshal," Giovanni adds as he drives, giving an approval for which nobody asked.

"I'd be sorry if a young, talented woman like her was in trouble," Palmieri says, hoping the Marshal will break his apparent confidentiality of investigations.

"Every rock star has troubles, just like any of us ordinary mortals, Sergeant," Alfredo says, bestowing half a statement.

"If you asked me to come off-duty, sir, I guess that yours was a courtesy tour. So, what do you think about Dark Mary?"

"I like her. I'm crazy about her, indeed."

"Like everybody. About her and her music as well."

"Oh, please, don't misunderstand me." Alfredo doesn't realize, yet, that Palmieri wants to know everything. This is not enough for her. But Alfredo's mouth seems so longing to talk. "The music Dark Mary plays doesn't engage me. I'm still in love with Bowie, Genesis, Led Zeppelin, and Deep Purple. And I only own *two* Black Sabbath records. Vinyl."

Palmieri turns back to look at Alfredo with a question mark on her face. Her fresh smell comes to the Marshal's nose, female in summertime vitality.

"Please, don't look at me like that, Sergeant. Since when ..." Alfredo says, and pauses, shifting his eyes to the running night on the Ostia pinewood, Cristoforo Colombo route. He holds the door handle. "Since I first saw that girl, my head's been a fucking mess. And now I've told everything you wanted to know, folks."

Palmieri laughs, clapping her hands.

Her boyfriend scolds the Sergeant. "C'mon, Cristina. Even a Marshal can fall in love, can't he?"

"You're right, Giovanni," Alfredo says, staring at the boy's eyes in the rearview mirror.

"Thank you, sir. The real fact is that women aren't used to hearing men talking straight about their feelings."

"Especially with men who aren't used to doing it. Not for a long time, my dear," Alfredo says, noticing – near the driver's head in the mirror – the headlights of a car tailing them.

That's strange.

"Sorry, Giovanni. Let me suggest you slow down. I think we've got speed cameras close ahead."

"Oh, fuck. Thank you, sir."

"Hey," Palmieri shouts.

"No problem, kids. But slow down," Alfredo says again, hoping to get the plate of the car behind them. "By the way. I guess I never told you about my little rock trick about Led Zeppelin, Deep Purple and Black Sabbath."

"No, sir. You never have. What's it about?" Palmieri asks.

"I've got the exclusive. It's the Rock Game of Spinning Vocals. A little thing, but pretty thrilling and disturbing. I've discovered it myself some time ago. But I will explain it back at the station, 'cause we need pen and paper, or a computer," Alfredo continues, keeping his eyes on the suspect car in the mirror. The driver slowing, just like their Opel. Then the car pulls over and stops while Giovanni – ignoring Alfredo's warning – keeps traveling at around eighty km/h. They leave the car back a good stretch; then Alfredo turns back to check, but the darkness shows nothing in particular.

"Oh, my God!" Palmieri screams.

Giovanni yells, "Fuck!" as he swerves.

Alfredo only sees – in black and white – a big tree heading toward the Opel hood.

Alfredo awakens alone on the ground.

Hands and face on cobblestones. He lifts his head, dazed, but recognizes one of the small streets of the Jewish Ghetto near his home.

"W-what?"

It's early-morning. Three o'clock. Somewhere in the shadows, there's the sound of running water. His precious watch at his wrist; smartphone, wallet and house keys still in his jacket pocket. Nobody has hit or robbed him. Instead, he's got something more now: a motherfucker headache. Alfredo stands, and he limps toward his flat. Just a few steps away from home. He realizes he was just in a car crash. He leans against the wall, tries to phone Sergeant Palmieri. It rings, but she doesn't answer.

Shit.

A car crash. Palmieri must have taken him home, unconscious.

But why was I on the ground?

Bad headache. He doesn't remember a fucking thing. A rivulet of blood rolls down his head, from his hair. It soaks one ear and drips on his neck.

Palmieri doesn't know where I live.

Three o'clock in the morning. It's too late – or too early – to wake the Captain, but Alfredo has no choice. He must tell him everything.

Alfredo's mobile rings. The display reads the name and number of Sergeant Palmieri.

Thank God.

"Cristina," Alfredo says with anxiety.

"No. It's Salvatores," the voice in the phone says.

Oh, shit. What should I tell him?

"Captain, I'm sorry. I thought it was the Sergeant. Where is she?"

"She's in front of me, Marshal. Sergeant Palmieri can no longer answer. We've lost her. I can hardly recognize her. Bad car crash with her fiancé along Cristoforo Colombo Street. The Sergeant went through the windshield and hit a tree. Dead on impact. No security belt. Bad habit. Where are you now, Marshal?"

"I …" he starts, too difficult to explain.

"You must tell me right now why you've called, in the thick of night, one of my officers not involved in your investigation. *Our* investigation, Marshal. You had to inform *me*."

"The reason is …" Alfredo says, pausing. "Personal, Captain, of course. That's all."

"We'll talk about this later. I need to let you know that the driver was saved by airbag and seatbelt. But it seems there was a third person aboard." Communication disturbance. "A third person who ran away after the crash."

I'll pay the price for my lie.

"The driver is dead, though: dismembered by one or your dog-men, apparently," the Captain booms.

"But this is not a full-moon night, Captain. And we've caught the wolf already," Alfredo states with relief. Stunned, he drags himself from alley to alley. Cockroaches run away from his every step.

"It's clear we have another on the loose, one who doesn't give a fuck about lunar phases."

A sense of loss paralyzes Alfredo at Costaguti square, under the window of his flat.

"As far as I know, it could be *you*, Marshal. Text messages on Palmieri's mobile show you had an appointment in Ostia, a Dark Mary show, then to come back together to Rome. With the car now pasted to the pine, here."

A lightning strike cracks inside Alfredo's mind, a subliminal frame impressed on his retina and then on the subconscious, a microsecond before the crash on Colombo Street: the headlights of the Opel against a humanoid wolf in the middle of the road.

"Now, tell me where you are, for God's sake," the Captain says.

"Yes, sir. I'm close to my flat, in the Jewish Ghetto. I was aboard their car. You don't let me talk, so it's very hard for me to explain," Alfredo says, guessing the RIS are already scanning repeaters to retrace all movements of his Nokia.

"How can you be in Rome without a vehicle if these two are dead on Colombo only minutes ago? Are you kidding me, Marshal?"

Alfredo screwed himself with his own hands. The Captain would have bought a lie, but Alfredo couldn't take the pressure.

"Captain, that's what I'm trying to figure out. I guess I lost consciousness. Maybe I came to after the crash and I hitchhiked. Maybe I fainted again while walking from the Tiber to my house," Alfredo says, faltering, dazed. "But I can't remember. Shit, I smashed my head. I'm bleeding, sir. What the fuck should I say? That I'm a werewolf and I let those two poor kids die? Or that I've put on my wings then passed through a pocket in the air? But what the fuck are we talking about?"

"All right, all right. I'll send a car and an ambulance."

"No, thank you. No need. I hate doctors anyway. I'm still alive. I'm talking, sir."

"Okay. Better you stick around, Marshal. Don't slip away. This whole thing is messing with my head. I just wish I could figure out how this fucking shit went down."

"I have got no reason to run, Captain. I'm Carabinieri, just like you. Keep your cool while I go home to dress my head wound. Damn it."

Mary took a foreigner, picking him up on Sant'Angelo Bridge, talking to him in German. He's pretty young, below forty, and he's quite drunk. The guy is alone and he seems to have lost his friends. She leads him down the Tiber banks, on the bicycle path. They have a walk while he keeps touching her everywhere. It's four o'clock in the morning. Lights paint the skyline like an upside-down oil on canvas over the calm waters of the stinky river. Mary and the German guy walk to a dark area where not even rats dare go. There is a staircase leading to a barred entrance. The marble banister and stairs are covered with trash, grass, dirty shreds. She makes him sit, mindlessly. He's out of order thanks to alcohol, so, despite the guy's libido, there'll be no erection that could threaten Mary. The German chicken seems boiled in lowest-price white wine. He probably drank while eating nothing at all. She undresses him out of a sweaty red T-shirt. The Kraut laughs like a child, feeling ashamed of showing his flabby pecs swinging like monkey tits. He tries to cover his chest with his hands. Mary moves his hands aside and he laughs more. The bad wine has melted his brain. He laughs and she hits his neck. He faints at once.

With her metal nails, Mary cuts the skin off his neck, until she finds his jugular vein. Skillfully, Mary stretches the large vessel, cuts it under his jaw and puts her mouth over the sliced end to receive the leaking blood in her dead stomach, as though his vein is a makeshift straw. Crouching over the man who is dying unconscious, Mary drinks his hot blood, shivering with pleasure as the red tissue of his jugular roughly rubs her inner mouth and throat.

Alcohol stuns her, too. The taste of iron climbs back, and some reflux, running through her, warming the outer layers of her skin that perspires ammonia. The bleeding process isn't complete. The little blood left inside the German makes the man die, after cerebral collapse, due to asphyxia. The viral proteolytic enzyme has already moved from Mary's mouth to the victim's organism. It's responsible for meta-death, producing the amino acids that will make the victim's tissues almost-alive. Contrary to the carrier, the victim's body dies, except for his heart, which stays alive and beating. Should Mary leave her victim whole, he would wake up in a sort of bio-automatism, having turned into a living dead, unaware and single-mindedly driven by primal instinct.

It's time to eat something. Slicing his solar plexus and flabby abdominal wall, Mary manually removes the Kraut's liver, ripping out rich portions. Her lips make disgusting noises as the morsels won't detach from fingers stained with blood. She chews and swallows quickly because she must take away the man's heart before dawn. Nobody must see; otherwise, she'll be forced to kill beyond necessity.

Now that Marshal is onto her, it's time to leave Rome and delay – somewhere else, sometime else – the end of her suffering. She weeps, tearing out the heart from the poor man's chest. As she always does with her victims, she leaves the body where she empties it. Mary cannot bury the body because the dead cannot put their counterpart underground. Only the living can hide the dead that way.

Dark Mary always wished her donors to stay hidden, to be destroyed by nature before anyone alive could discover them. But clearly, her strategy failed.

Death piles up over life.

And never the opposite.

Death is appearance that doesn't cheat.

Like the hearts she infects, pulsating in her hands instead of dying with the fleshy homes from which they came.

Four o'clock in the morning.

Alfredo has reached his flat.

Turned off all the lights.

On the lookout at his window, his mind rambles because whoever took him back to the ghetto knows where he lives.

Dark Mary and that beautiful woman behind me. That woman watches over Mary. She protects her. She's her accessory. They've come after me and Palmieri with that car I saw behind ours. A wolf killed poor Giovanni after the crash. Why didn't it kill me, too? Who's taken me here? Mary and the wolf? How could they know I live here? That woman at the beach, is she the wolf who protects Mary? Or is Mary protecting her?

"Jesus."

A light noise.

Alfredo turns back and takes a look at the main door, which has moved on the hinges within its wooden frame, even locked. A gust of wind, perhaps.

But the air is still tonight.

The Marshal stays at the window, unmoving. He stares at the dark, not breathing, waiting for a replica of the noise he randomly heard in the silence. He stays, without swallowing, until the vertebrae of his neck seem to petrify in that position, until he realizes he's been in apnea for maybe two minutes. His temples drumming like double gun hammers.

A growl.

Shit.

The tone is low, like a tiger's. It sounds like a rotor slowly spinning, a guttural sound from a deep throat. Alfredo silently takes off his shoes. He gets down on all fours. The wooden floor creaks under his weight.

There's a wolf behind the fucking door. We have jackshit arrested. Werewolves exist, I've seen them, holy shit, and I've got no silver stuff on me.

He crawls slowly, pausing every few seconds.

Why don't I own half a fucking silver pen?

A short growl. For a second, it seems to reverberate among the books.

It's not a werewolf; it's a lycanthrope. Lycanthropes can change at will, with or without a full moon. I've only captured wolf-men. Is this the wolf who's killed Giovanni tonight?

Alfredo lies down on the floor. He levels his gaze through door and ground.

Only darkness.

And the weak blow in his face of cool, moldy air from the landing.

Nobody can stop Dark Mary because she's protected by a wolf. Dark Mary can confess her crimes on the radio because there's a wolf who watches over her. Someone affected by terianthropy. The same who knows where I live and who wants to do me in and keep protecting Mary.

The thin snarl, long as it is calm, now shakes the air.

But it doesn't come from outside.

It's behind me.

Mary smells him at the front doors.

Things precipitate. An apparent sign of collapse. A baleful declaration of war. It seems the world is coming down on her head more so than ever.

Antonio, the old, fat baker … he was going back home after work, still covered in flour.

Martyna took him by surprise, dragged him in the dark basement downstairs. She sliced him open, devoured the flesh of his legs, neck, sides, and shoulders. With her claws, he worked on his waistline, making a skirt of bowels drop over his legs; he died sitting on them.

Poor Antonio.

He'd given Mary kilos of bread over the years, ignoring that she couldn't eat a crumble.

Mary doesn't need light to see the blood spatters in that basement. The deejay must hurry to put an end to all that. Martyna seems to have dramatically decided to make things worse. She takes the drill out of her flight case, a Bosch Psr 12. It's pretty silent, but she knows well that the few residents are luckily heavy sleepers. A dozen holes will be enough to make his head explode when the dead changes into a wolf. She cannot kill him in person; her own feeding is already an infinite burden of guilt. But it'd be harmful to let the wolf spread its spawn, an ungovernable breed that kills only in the name of anarchy and narcissism.

The old baker, Antonio, receives the drilling. He bleeds, exhaling a spindly shriek under Mary's hands, and a stink of burnt bone.

"Thank you for all the bread, my friend."

THE OLD WOMAN, THE PRIEST, THE HEART AND HIS LADY: 6TH OF AUGUST

"You must not behave like this, Susanna," Father Sebastiano whispers.

He's on his knees in tears and despair, holding tiny Mirella tightly. She's lifeless, a look of terror on her face. Her soul has teetered on the edge of the unknown. This is what Sebastiano can read in the eyes of the dead as he touches her hair. It's very clear to him that this is his fault. His rage forces him not to raise his eyes to the woman who's killed the old landlady.

Susanna faces the priest's reproach with no reaction. Wearing her checkered outfit, her arms hang to her sides. She stands motionless in the corridor without making a move. Only absorbing Sebastiano's anger.

"You have no brain. You can't think or ponder, only obey," Sebastiano states.

She reaches out to the priest's head. All of a sudden, she grabs his hair and pulls him to her. If she squeezes just a little more, the man's scalp will tear away like wet paper.

"I've molded you with the clay of the souls I devoured," the priest says, grinning. "You are the child of God's children, from whom I took the spirit before it went back being holy." He's known far worse torments. He clutches Susanna's wrists and pushes his fingers inside her flesh of living dirt. All that Sebastiano has coughed out his lungs, now a Promethean evidence, compacted and modeled into human shape with partial mental capacity. Up until now, Susanna had behaved like an infant. Sebastiano couldn't foresee this. "I did not create you for my amusement. You are only a medium, a converter, useful for a worthier creature of God," the priest says, lifted from the floor by the monster.

In the dark, he can see the vacuous light from the depth of her eyes.

The woman moves her mouth of black clay. Her oral cavity is full of matter unable to express words. Sebastiano reads an obscene litany of blasphemies on the primitive labial speech of Susanna.

"I close my eyes not to listen," Sebastiano fiercely mutters. And trying to think about how to tame the living tower.

Susanna lets the priest go, letting him drop on the floor at her feet beside the dead Mirella. She leans down in a clumsy, stiff movement, this time grabbing the priest's neck with her large fingers.

"I command you to leave me, and to be completely still," Sebastiano shouts in a wire of strangled voice.

From Susanna static, vertical face, a gaze of cold hatred shines. Father Sebastiano drives his fingers in to poke the clay-giant's eyes. "You don't deserve sight. You don't deserve hearing. You don't deserve to talk and curse the name of the Father who's not yours," the priest states, coughing after a breath. The contact with the woman made of soul scraps has soiled him.

Sebastiano gets up on his feet to stir Susanna's features. He modifies the creature's soft matter, the ducts that can influence and drive her basic will: her eyes and mouth. Re-molding her face, the priest seems to have solved the problem of taming his female golem. Now she only has a nose and ears, only able to listen and obey his orders without thinking.

"You will walk by holding my hand and following my voice, if you don't want me to saw your legs, Susanna."

The woman of clay rests her arms at her sides. She stands there, waiting further commands from her master.

"Never, ever, would I think to take the place of our Lord God, Susanna. My task has a single, noble purpose; your form of life depends on that, and it will end with its accomplishment. After that, you'll have to be destroyed."

Her chest doesn't breathe. Her belly doesn't pulsate. Susanna utters a mysterious thought, turning her head from right to the left and back again. Maybe she's saying *no*. The priest feels a knock of sadness.

"Now I can tell that you're infused with a sort of life. That's a prodigy and a good omen, too. I guess you're ready," the priest says, taking Susanna by hand.

He leads her back to the dining room, where Mirella saw her just before dying. The porphyria-sick priest leaves her in there. After several productive coughs, he walks back to the hall.

"Mirella," he whispers, as he crouches beside the woman. "*Ego te benedico in nomine patris et filii et spiritus sancti. Amen.*"

Sebastiano sheds a tear. He shuts the woman's eyelids and mouth. Then he takes her in his arms and says a Hail Mary, softly cradling her.

Standing in the middle of the room is Susanna, probably looking at them with her smooth, eyeless face. No judgment, no triggering will. She only hears the priest's words.

Mirella's hands are furrowed and clawed. Her blood shifts down to the lower areas of her body, as her heart has stopped, draining weight and color from her raised part, from her face and shoulders.

Sebastiano isn't afraid of death, but this time a chilling breeze blows inside him because he's late to drink Mirella's soul.

So now, for the very first time, he feels lonely.

He returns Mirella to her home. He carries the old lady to her bed before going back out. He closes the door, blesses the house.

Back in his apartment, with the first light of day, Sebastiano can begin his ritual.

After undressing her, he pronounces basic orders to make Susanna lie on the table behind her. Now the clay golem is naked, completely black and slimy with her sandy bitumen.

Sebastiano takes the elected heart, the chosen one. He had smuggled it inside a glass jar, covered by a black cloth, and brought it home in his leather bag. From the underground maze, until this moment, the cardiac muscle has seen no sunlight, so it's pure, immaculate. The living motion picture of its owner's life is whole, and it's spinning from atria to ventricles with electric concentricity.

"We're ready, Susanna. You are ready."

Sebastiano crosses both his elements: Susanna and the beating heart inside the jar.

Holy water in a blessed carafe.

Sterilized linen cloths to clean up and dry himself once the operation is finished.

A prayer, then a hymn from the Psalms.

A few candles and a little statue of the Virgin Mother Mary, her hands open over Susanna's head.

The gifted heart beats. From the face of its muscular surface, in never-ending contraction, comes a dull arrhythmia of joy that seems to be ringing.

Susanna's body spreads the same smell of Sebastiano's mouth. Susanna is Sebastiano's sister in saliva, having lived inside his lungs in shameful form.

"God, please, bless us and forgive our sins. Amen."

The little flames of the candles point the same direction. It's the pulsing heart, drawing the energy of their little fires.

Sebastiano twists open the jar lid, then he tries to grab and pull out the muscle. It's greased with gluey sweat, and slips away from the priest's nervous fingers, his emotion growing as he touches the imperious beating of the living flesh. It flits in his hand like a fish out of water as Sebastiano digs his fingers into Susanna's warm chest. "You are ready to receive it."

The hole is large enough.

Little more than a fist.

Sebastiano blesses the recess in the dirt chest of his creature, which is waiting for the human gift.

The priest sets the heart inside, then he carefully buries it.

Susanna sustains the installation without shifting limbs.

Sebastiano molds the clay chest of his golem as she lies on the table.

Once finished, he sits beside the mute woman and rests on a chair, waiting for the shadows of the night to watch over his creature until daylight.

DIASTEMA

"I should kill him," Martyna says.

"Do it, and you'll die," Mary promises.

"I'm tired of your incessant attempts to run from me. We're tied to one another. Don't pretend you've forgotten."

"Martyna. You're sick with jealousy. Your feeling is unreal, and insane. Nothing acceptable. It has nothing left of what seduced me, at the time. Our relationship cannot rest on your foolish need to love me at all costs. So, please, love somebody else."

"You're a neurotic little dead thing that reasons like a pendulum clock. You can only swing between two ideas. Escaping me, and thinking about yourself. That's what your wonderful time-beat actually comes down to. Besides basic daily bullshit, no longer involving me, of course."

"You're jealous even of the air I breathe, of what I see and what I think. You're even jealous of what I eat, Martyna."

"Shit. I am not jealous; only human beings live for such foolish things." Martyna smiles, sits on the dining room couch. "Just like that Marshal who's onto you now. All the fans weren't enough; now you've got artillery, too."

"It was to be expected. Our way of life cannot stay unseen for long. That is, unless I could evolve my natural abilities," Mary says.

"And so you waste your time doing the musician. First of all, you must be a perfect nomen."

"At last, you're right, Marty. I still cannot be a perfect nomen, and that's because I met you. With you by my side, everything gets complicated. Just take a look at what you did to the old baker. Was that necessary?"

"I've got to eat, too, don't I?"

"Go and do it elsewhere. Not here, in my house."

"This is my home, too, darling," Martyna protests.

Dark Mary snarls at her. "No longer. Didn't you leave the night I broke your bones? Did you forget that? It seems you're still here."

Martyna laughs at her from the couch. She adds an ironic, significant gesture, as though she took no part in the matter.

Mary goes on. "The police will find the baker's body in here, if the old man is late in waking up and moving away by himself."

"It was your idea, Mary, that bullshit of taking the Marshal back home after the crash. What's with all the goodwill now? That jerk wants to catch you and you help him out?" Martyna shouts, drooling. "But you wanted to do it your own way, threatening me as usual. So we carry him in our car, leave him on the street. Maybe we should've also shaven him, dressed his hair, right? What bullshit, Mary."

Mary listens to her in silence.

"But I read his thoughts," Martyna continues, "and that hound got it all. So it's up to you to face the consequences."

"Interesting. When did you read his thoughts, if he was unconscious?"

"While you were busy with the baker. I prepared him for you, expressly to that end, so I had time to pay a visit to the Marshal ... who was still awake."

"You went after him?"

"We took him back home together, honey. As you requested. It won't take long for that jerk to figure out we know where he lives – damn, we're across the street. I didn't kill him because I wanted you to understand how stupid you are, and how much you need me."

A slap of awareness, right in the face. Humiliating. Mary can only blink. Stunned.

Martyna begins to snarl, bloody smoke blowing out her nostrils. "So, I'm going to kill him right now. Before dawn."

"It's all falling apart. Badly. And it's your fault. I must leave this place, Martyna. I must leave Rome. And, most of all ..."

Martyna writhes in a feast of violent spasms as her hypophysis discharges endorphins and morphological hormones throughout her body. Bone elements multiply, muscle masses clone, redoubling as programmed by the genetic score. The woman orders her wild side to take over her whole structure.

"I must be free of you, Martyna."

As she shape-shifts, Dark Mary dilutes in her sight. The woman-wolf sees her lover in a sort of golden painting. The rage generated by her sad words, by that grim scenario, makes her even angrier.

It's me *who must be free of* you, *Mary.*

Alfredo has a headache.

It's not neuralgia; his pineal gland is working hard, like a running train engine.

If the wolf has found me, I guess it's because it can watch over me. Time to see what's behind the window.

The wolf will be back, but Alfredo has found his silver fountain pen.

He had watched at the window of the attic across the street for hours, hidden behind the curtains. If the wolf really lives inside that flat, he can wait for it to turn into human shape again, and then arrest him. *Or her.* And anyone he's going to find in there will be forced to take medical tests, to discover perhaps a second animal nature, and at the cost of deporting all the residents of the building to the Military Hospital, throwing them all in observation cells.

The old building of the baker is almost deserted; almost all the families – belonging to the same Jewish bloodline – are gone. The empty apartments have not been rented out, nor sold to unrelated people. Time stands still, inside there.

Vanacura goes out.

Passing through the main door, the Marshal jumps back to the early twentieth century.

The soft light of the night weakly enters through the glass door. But this is not a problem for the Marshal. His ability to smell can focus on what his eyes sense in the shadow. Stains on the floor.

Blood. Fresh.

Footprints on the stairs, coming from the dark basement.

The Marshal looks up the stairwell; from there, he hears heavy steps climbing with difficulty.

Better grab the gun.

Those shoes, soaked with blood, are going up.

A man. Injured. Unsteady.

The Marshal counts floors as he rises without a sound: first, second, third, fourth, and fifth.

The stranger stopped at the attic. Fuck.

Alfredo reaches the fourth floor when that man finishes his climb.

Time seems frozen, like space, inside that old building.

Screams break the silence.

When the wolf screams, it means it's seeing its painful birth again. Martyna's mind runs back to her distant past as she shape-shifts.

Sixty seconds in the wolf's mind, like a ritual nightmare, every time she turns.

The memories lead her again in the house where Matthew took her, in the Sproul forest. Memory shows her awakening naked and tied to a table in the afternoon light. She's in a house, not hers, and not Matt's either. The table is a sort of altar in a living room packed with books, candles, skulls, stuffed animals, severed mummified hands, goat heads, and snakes nailed to the walls.

Close to her, there's a man apparently waiting for her to awaken. It's that nut-head Gohen. A large, paper-bag mask on his head. A *South Park* face drawn around the eye-holes in marker. His black, three-pointed beard hangs below, long and bristly and filthy on his pale, fat, sweaty chest. Maybe that jerk thinks nobody could recognize him. Suddenly, Martyna focuses on the five-pointed star scarification on his torso. She never saw that before. She believes it's a prank … after the violence in the funeral home lab, no doubt. She starts to scream Matthew's name, pulling at the leather straps handcuffing her to the altar, sawing into her skin.

Matthew is not there; he's not coming. From the floor, around the altar, stand a bunch of other priests. They're hooded, naked, scraped, and bleeding, and they close in around her as their bearded master Gohen orders.

Someone starts a pipe-organ, a monotonous tune – some record player – while the air is already burnt with candles and incense smoke. Gohen recites incomprehensible propitiatory formulas.

This is unreal. Must be some kind of punishment arranged by that bastard moron Matthew.

She has no idea what's happening. Maybe her boyfriend has conceived this masquerade to complete the awful initiation begun among the dead in his funeral lab. Maybe that asshole will come over drunk, jump on the altar and do some crazy things to her. The sect remains assembled until someone arrives. Not Matthew, but a shadow beheading one of the followers with a fast blow of its arm. Proving this is not some sort of joke. The blood splattering Martyna's tits makes her heart, and her screams, suddenly stop. A never-sensed, feral stench smashes her nose, giving her vertigo. The grotesque presence is a sort of human spruce of black fur. Martyna tries not to faint. She must stay awake.

The special guest is so tall that its head brushes the ceiling, stinky and wild. Not a man, because of its fur, though it can't be an ape, but neither a bear. With long claws, it had severed a man's head. Eyes and fangs that blaze in the moist darkness of its coat. Its arms are long and covered with plenty of hair, and its breathing makes a sound like a rope running through the hole in a cardboard box. The thing does not seem to have a face, because even the light seems afraid to touch its features. It leans closely over Martyna, and finally she sees clearly. The head of the special guest has a wrinkled, grey face, like that of a canine-chimp hybrid, and with round completely black eyes, like a tarantula's.

The beast smells her face while she shakes and mutters *oh my god oh god oh my* out of fear. She feels her heart breaking. She's paralyzed.

Gohen's followers, and he as well, are petrified behind its back. Martyna isn't able to wonder what the connection could be between this group of idiots and the beast. All she can do is pray for God to let her die, and soon, with the least amount of pain.

In an unspoken plea, Martyna turns to look at Gohen, but he seems disoriented by the beast's hesitation. Seeing that he is trembling, too, is little consolation.

Gohen has offered Martyna in sacrifice, it seems, but the beast looks like it's thinking about something different behind its spidery eyes.

It suddenly bites Martyna's arm.

A twitch, like the hit of a scorpion tail.

Then, the thing vanishes in the darkest corner of the house, emptying the living room and smothering the horror of its summoning.

Gohen unmasks himself and orders his servants to do the same.

Everyone watches Martyna writhing with aches and spasms.

A strong geyser of dark blue liquid, coming from a fire in her belly, spits out from Martyna's mouth. The fluid splatters her naked body, shaken by fierce cramps from head to toe.

One by one, and pale with fear, the priests move behind their master. Perhaps they were expecting a bloody mess, or a messy rape – as it may have already happened on that same altar.

Everyone seems unprepared, and terrified. Perhaps they thought the beast would kill the girl, as it did with the other sacrifices.

Now Martyna is having a fit, throwing up blood and black stuff, some bile with red clots. Her muscles mindlessly dart as though they wish to escape from her skin as her bones roar in pain. When the fit is over, Martyna lets out her very first growl.

She rips out of the handcuffs.

Stands on the altar on powerful legs.

For some seconds, she watches the pack of brats from above.

Then she dives on them, her strength increased hundredfold.

She wants to scratch one, but in a single blow slices open two of them with her claws. Their bellies are like blossoming flowers of bowels, their faces trapped in childish wonder.

The smell of blood makes her rage burst: a form of excitement, a turmoil in her stomach, and a slimy stream from her pussy and down her legs.

No mercy for those poor cretins.

Her arms are quick propellers that make the naked bodies around her deflagrate. The living room turns into a centrifuge of blood and shredded flesh. Her teeth itch inside her gums – not her brain asking to bite and bite, but the teeth – to calm the crazy burning of the nerves of her mouth. Her fury grows ever more, and more, until her mind turns blank from a deafened rumble.

The memory-movie changes, and takes her out of Gohen's cabin. There are woods, now, deep in the night, and not wind shaking the trees but the screams of the men leaving this world having seen the devil in their final seconds.

At dawn, Martyna finds herself among a triumph of slaughtered flesh in the house, which is already invaded by flies. She remembers everything. She cannot believe what she had done, but won't run away from the massacre, for she has only defended herself. Her mind is clear. She needs to wash away the blood covering her entire body, from her feet to her hair, blood that chokes her as it dries and pulls at her skin. She's dying from thirst. She must look for water.

She finds a brook nearby, hidden in the woods. She's naked and alone, but feels no fear. She washes, and drinks in the heart of the forest.

Air is her only dress, now, and her thoughts float in the nothingness of pure peace with nature all around. Her mood is light, shining with one set of desires: tearing Matthew apart, destroying him, devouring him alive, and making his heart explode, thus crushing his entire existence.

The following nights, her body dresses with fury, playing again at slaughtering the already-dead flesh inside Gohen's house, teaching her senses about the new food in a prehistoric journey through blood, through taste and smell, until she's able to find in the woods the stink of her returning man.

The start of her first hunt.

She chases, she stalks, she devours Matt.

And, with that, the sixty cardiac seconds of the shape-shifting process close the loop of the memory-movie, and Martyna is a wolf again.

The wolf's back scrapes the ceiling as it pounces on Dark Mary.

Alfredo springs like a jack-in-the-box at the wolf's scream from the highest flat. He runs upstairs, to the attic, and finds Antonio, the baker, standing in a strange syncope in front of the door from which new, fierce roars emanate.

"Antonio," Alfredo shouts. "Antonio, get away."

He struggles to climb the last steps and hurries across the landing. The old baker wears a white undershirt and blue pants, all soaked in blood. The Marshal sees only his back, but quickly determines the wolf has slashed him open like a pig. His guts coil around his feet. Lazily, the baker turns his head to him, as though wishing to see what the anxious voice at his back wants with him. The man seems in a sort of half-slumber. The massive gashes on his face shine brightly of living flesh.

The Marshal is shocked by another detail, though: the man's head is drilled.

Sounds of struggle from inside the flat.

Alfredo pushes Antonio aside, shoots the lock and enters.

"Mary," he shouts.

The two women are in front of him, one almost recognizable.

Martyna is gigantic and statuesque, despite her folded knees. Black fur sticks up like porcupine quills on her hump. She growls, opens her jaws, pulling her lips back to reveal fangs and all her drooling rage. Her powerful arms shake and rip Mary apart on the floor beneath her.

A shocking lack of blood.

Aim at the forehead, Fildor says within Alfredo's mind and hand. *Then, shoot.*

Alfredo pulls the trigger.

The Martyna-wolf's head explodes, splattering plasma, bone, and brain crumbles around the room, even on the ceiling. With spastic shudders, the lycanthrope flexes backward – showing eight flabby tits – and drops to its knees, crashing to the floor with its undone head. Death crystallizes the creature in a stiff arch as its features fade, revealing the colors and shape of a woman.

The transformation gives Alfredo a sense of vertigo.

Is my job already done here?

Mary lies on the floor, brushing the hems of her wounds. She weeps in a desperate assault of joy.

Glancing back, he finds Antonio still behind him – confused, speechless, eyes lost in amnesia – and looking for something, perhaps water to quench the bowels wrapped around his feet. The baker heads for the bathroom.

Alfredo follows him, searching for the silver pen in his pocket. It's a fountain pen with a wide point. With his other hand, he returns the Beretta to his jacket pocket. He takes off the pen cap, holds it like a knife. He gets closer to the old baker's shoulders, and then jabs it in, stabbing him in the neck through a large cut left by the wolf's nails. Alfredo sinks the pen its entire length. The old man slows his step. He stumbles, unsteady, and opens the bathroom door. From the window, the light of dawn. A few steps more and he stops, collapses facedown, spreading his bowels all around his lifeless body.

"Mary," Alfredo whispers, returning to her and crouching beside the meta-dead.

"It's nothing, Marshal," Dark Mary says, smiling as she rests on the floor. "These wounds, dreadful as they may appear, will close up soon."

Alfredo admires her shredded body, her plowed meat that doesn't spit blood. Her open, dead flesh expels an evaporation that hurts the eyes, an acid steam of methane and nitrogen.

"I couldn't protect my wolf any longer, Marshal. You can't protect that which wants to destroy you."

"It's the same old problem that must face anybody who wants to live in this filthy world, Mary," Alfredo mutters, caressing her hair. He glances at the wolf-woman, curved in a human wheel back on her spine; against the light from the window, she looks like a sculpture emerged from the hereafter, a bare olive tree twisted on itself.

"She was a great photographer of corpses. But her mind depicted unbridgeable sorrows, feeding on a curse that was only curable with death – the death she ever glorified through art."

"Mary, I –"

"Don't need to say it, Marshal," she whispers, her wounds gurgling loudly as they heal. "I know your thoughts."

"Don't need to say what?" he asks, worried, laying on his side and dangerously close to Mary's petite body.

"That's impossible, Marshal. Don't try to kiss me. It's enough to turn you into what I'm tired of being."

"I'm already infected with sadness, depression, and dismay. I only have to think you away."

"I won't leave this house, but I will come back only when everything has changed. When no one is able to ask what you discovered about me."

"Mary, I am already protecting you."

"I know. But danger will come looking for you. Not me."

Down on the street, the buzz of a Carabinieri car.

Alfredo looks out the window, but can't see the square or the window of his own flat. He tries from the kitchen, then from the room with the bathtub. But weirdly, the only room with view of his flat is the little bathroom where the old baker had died. Too small ... and doesn't seem to be directly in front of his own window.

What. The. Fuck.

THE CAPTAIN, THE MARSHAL, THE LYCANTHROPE, AND THE BAKER

Two o'clock, p.m.

"Thank you, Marshal. I sincerely apologize for my call this morning. I was out of my head," Captain Salvatores says. Then, he sighs. "Our poor Sergeant Palmieri."

"Don't worry about me, Captain," Alfredo says. "It was a tragic story that put all of us under strain. Miss Palmieri has not died in vain. Thanks to her, we stopped the massacre *and* the contagion."

"So, now. What are you going to do, Marshal?" the Captain asks, returning to his car.

"I guess I'll have a smoke."

Martyna exits the old building on Costaguti square inside an aluminum coffin.

Antonio, the old owner of the ancient ghetto bakery, follows her aboard the Mortuary truck.

It's a nondescript August afternoon.

THE MARSHAL, THE BOOK, THE WINDOW, AND THE MOTHER: 4TH OF SEPTEMBER. 10:28 P.M.

Obsessed by the window of the attic – where the short battle against the lycanthrope ended – Alfredo has feverishly waited for the next full moon, reading tales of terror by Edgar Allan Poe, as his pineal gland requested.

Going back over those stories has led to further suspicion about Mary's house.

Some days have passed since the full moon cycle.

Potential victims of a wolf on the loose could lay scattered across the wild areas of the city. But one thing is certain: nobody came snarling at his back.

But that fucking window ...

It's trying to tell him something.

The attic window doesn't match with any of the rooms I scoped.

He puts on a shirt while some kind of phone rings inside his brain. Again, and again.

That window is the view from a hidden room.

Nobody saw him pass through the main door.

Nobody heard him going upstairs again, to the door where the old living-dead baker had halted with his guts at his feet.

Alfredo rips through the Carabinieri Corps seals.

Then he enters, holding a flashlight, his pipe in his mouth.

Only now does he realize he's hurried out wearing plastic slippers.

Clear-headed, he tries to get his bearings and makes a map of the flat, relative to the window of his own. The last time here he only had a quick look at the windowless bedroom. This time, Alfredo finds the room empty, heavy with stagnant air. And, no windows.

This room is shorter than the others.

Alfredo hurries toward the wall in front of him, beyond the bed surrounded by candelabras and spatters of rusty blood. A real deathbed.

The room that should *be in front of my flat has a wall, instead of the window I see from mine.*

Alfredo knocks on the wall. It sounds empty.

With his flashlight, he finds the light switch and turns it on. On the floor is an iron rod, ready to use. The plasterboard offers no resistance as Alfredo breaks through the wall with calculated strikes.

Through the hole he makes, a dry stench blows in the Marshal's face. He almost faints with nausea. Two coughs, and then he widens the hole with his hands, enough to aim the flashlight inside and take a look inside. Beyond is a small empty room, and the window seen from his flat, with wooden planks bolted on its frame.

Oh, shit. It's not empty at all.

On an old wicker chair, a mummified woman sits at the window.

Her gown and coiffure date her death around the early 1900s. Her dry lips are pulled back, baring teeth.

I don't see spider webs. And not a veil of dust on the hidden woman's shoulders, nor on her hair. But there *is* dust around her feet.

Dark Mary's voice echoes in Alfredo's mind, then, the only useful sentence: *I will persecute you psychically, just like my mother still does with me.*

And Alfredo answers: *If this woman is still alive, she doesn't have the strength to open her eyes.*

Or maybe she's only sleeping ...

VESPERS OF HEARTS

Sebastiano says Mass.

Mary has stopped coming to him.

He's purified the chosen heart, having implanted it within Susanna's chest.

Mary was supposed to take that purified heart for herself. She needed it for a transplant, the only way to return human. And mortal. She could have died, one day, sooner or later, but in peace.

What if she had carried the Norwegian girl's heart in her chest?

Maybe she would have sensed it beating the euthanasia of their love until the end of her days.

But now, Sebastiano can no longer extract that heart from the golem's chest; neither can he leave it inside that fake body.

God is not telling him what could happen; that handful of faithful praying, and listening, ignore what lies ahead for Sebastiano, now, at home.

A STRANGE KIND OF MAN

Sixty seconds to leave Mary's attic. Sixty seconds to go downstairs and back home. Sixty seconds and the Marshal's memory accompanies him, showing him his own story.

Some years ago.

It's seven in the morning, a filthy morning on the narrow alleys of the Spanish Quarters of Naples.

At the time, Alfredo isn't a Marshal yet, but a Carabinieri Sergeant.

He's fatally alone in Tofa Alley, near Santissima Trinità degli Spagnoli church, and handcuffing a facedown Camorra killer he has chased there.

That's when he feels the barrel of a P38 pressed against his head.

Alfredo must choose: free the killer – hoping not to be killed anyway – or to quickly say a prayer. As soon as he tries to turn toward the accomplice, however, the enigma solves itself. The P38 fires. Alfredo sees a white light, like a hot wire spinning around his head in a circle of fire, and then he collapses facedown on the ground.

Assunta, Alfredo's mother, seems sixty years old forever. She's a Nazi Lager survivor, having seen her husband leaving as ashes through the smokestacks. She can take the presence of bodies, but she's only a few steps away from no longer being able to say that she's seen *everything* in her life.

Assunta is coming back home from shopping, carrying many bags. She decides to take the long way and drop by Santissima Trinità to say a prayer for her husband Umberto, burnt in the Nazi furnaces just this day of the year; that's when she hears the sound of a gunshot from Tofa. The harsh sound echoes across the alley while the rest of Naples seems to be swallowed in temporary emptiness. Assunta sees a man down, and a bluish smoke floating in the air between the black façade of the buildings. Despite the laundry hanging from the balconies, it suddenly seems as if nobody lives there.

She has no doubt that God has led her there in time to see that someone has shot her son. Without dropping her heavy shopping bags, Assunta hurries toward Alfredo.

He lies face down in a spreading puddle of dark fluid, like petroleum. She gets closer, above him. She cannot kneel because of rheumatisms, but sees the river of blood spilling from her son's head.

Alfredo, she whispers.

Mom, Alfredo murmurs, frowning as though awakened from an after-lunch nap. *What a headache*, he says in an unsteady voice.

While Assunta looks around to see if someone is lurking, Alfredo rises, and dons his legendary hat. A red blood mask covers his face.

Mother and son, face to face, stare at each other.

The man sways a bit, as if under the influence of Valium.

Where are you going, Mom? Home is the other way. Give me those bags, he grumbles, cleaning his face with a handkerchief. *You look worried. What's wrong?*

I'm not worried at all. It's your job.

Give me the bags.

Nope, his mother replies.

But they're too heavy. Give them to me, Alfredo insists.

A drop of blood quivers on the tip of his nose.

I just wanted to say an Eternal Rest for your father, but it seems you need it more than he does.

How many times did he ask for those bags?

A million?

The Marshal smiles at that memory now, switching his gaze to the present.

Ten years have passed.

Having risen to his feet, after being shot in the head – the bullet making a mysterious, underskin ring around his head instead of piercing the skull – may be a story nobody else in the world can tell.

Living and working in the pigsty of Rome is more relaxing.

Alfredo is on the rolling tram number 8, running toward Torre Argentina square. He enjoys the sun through the large windows.

Nothing better than sitting on a tram with the sun on your face.

He's just had dinner with his mother. She came back to Rome, a few days ago, after a long cruise along the Nile. With her, he'd relaxed. The meal was good, and he spent a nice evening smoking his pipe on the porch. He didn't talk about bodies and the living-dead, and not about people sick with rabies and *canine transitory acromegaly*. He didn't even talk about Mary, a stinging regret.

According to his Jewish heritage, he's also sorry of being so ill-disposed toward Indian, Philippine, and Chinese folks in the city. Not out of racism, but epidemiological factors.

One of his most oppressive paranoias.

A sad, livid fear of bacteria weighs on his chest, a sort of panic attack whenever it takes over. Trams have always been the vehicle of choice for ethnic minorities. Eastern people aren't used to the climate of Rome, so they catch colds and bronchitis easily. They are always last to jump on and off the tram, making the driver mad every time. And those disease-spreaders touch every banister, every stop-button, greasing them with snot after blowing noses in their hands.

After that shot in the head, Alfredo was forced to give up driving because of a significant loss of visual field. He's bound to move around via public transport – those pay wards on wheels of respiratory plagues – so he can observe the behaviors of a population who thinks itself unseen. The strangers infect the city. Every public place crawls with bacteria and germs, colonies of pathogens.

The city of seven ills.

Every passenger leaves the tram or train or bus after an invisible viral bath, after having inhaled the breath and cough of the Eastern, the spreaders of the never-ending flu.

The Marshal is not a racist; he's only dramatically worried. If public transportation is made of urban oil-tankers of bacteria, the population packed in ever-smaller spaces becomes the most prolific lab for a new strain of influenza.

New genetic mutations of respiratory germs.

Even the dogs, damn.

Even dogs take the bus, and breathe with open mouths their haul of virus, maybe carrying ticks and fleas. A single tick is enough. A single flea is enough. One tick jumps onto your leg. You scratch yourself, accidentally break the insect, and you will infect your own blood with the toxins spread by the crushed parasite stuck in your skin. So you go into anaphylactic shock. Then, there are the infants. They cough and sneeze with open mouths. Each is maybe incubating an infectious disease that can bring heavy complications to an adult.

All these are obsessions Max Fildor attached to his mind like stickers. Racial contamination must mean something. Xenophobic feelings have a purpose, after all; they help *to hide.*

If the living-death is a sort of virus, it probably causes rabies and hostile moods. This way, everybody is busy watching over strangers and giving them every social shame.

The traditional citizen loses identity, hidden among the growing number of African, Eastern, and Russian people.

Italians are always silent aboard buses and trams.

How many are the living, and how many could be the dead?

"Please, I'm getting down here," Alfredo mutters to Russians crowding the door.

The Marshal climbs off the tram. He's not sure if he's going home or looking for something at the Feltrinelli bookstore.

Time to find some new music records.

Red light. He must wait.

He takes the phone out of his pocket, and sends a message to his Captain.

Captain, good evening. I'm going to take a few days off. Going for a trip. I'll call you tomorrow, in the morning. Alfredo Vanacura.

The Marshal's eyes remain glued to the phone display, reading his last name several times.

Alfredo Vanacura

ƨ ƨ ƨ

A chubby, red-haired guy wearing mirrored Ray-Ban glasses approaches. The stranger laughs at him for no apparent reason.

PART FOUR
PIERCING

Red light, green light. Alfredo crosses the street.

Suddenly, his entire world flies away from his sight, everything upside-down. After some seconds, he hears a clash of broken glass and metal.

Did they run me over?

A rush of heat all over his right side, the left turning cold quickly.

Oh, yes. I'm really flying.

Alfredo tries to rise in the middle of Vittorio Emanuele Avenue, the street going from Torre Argentina square to Sant'Angelo Bridge.

A gathering crowd surrounds him.

The Marshal picks up his hat, puts it on.

The Marshal's been run over.

Where's the fucking pain?

Alfredo takes his phone from the ground. It still works.

They look terrified *of* him, screaming, as if insane.

His torso abruptly bends on a side while calling. He's standing still, but his upper half is weirdly folded downward. Alfredo's world is totally overturned.

Everyone is screaming at the sight. People scream and faint.

"Hello?" Assunta answers.

"Mom, it's Alfredo. Just wanted to tell you I'm leaving for a trip."

"That's good, Alfredo. Have a nice time. Please, call me when you're back. Don't make me worry, as usual."

"Of course, Mom," Alfredo promises as he begins to walk,

broken in two.

"You know, I still have to tell you a lot of things about the Nile," she adds.

"Mom ..." Blood dribbles on Alfredo's mouth.

"Tell me, honey."

"Mom, I forgot to tell you. I've fallen in love with a woman."

"Me too, Alfredo."

THE AUTHOR

PAOLO DI ORAZIO is an author of horror fiction and comics books, whose work has been published in Italian since 1987, including novels, short and long fiction, collections and scripts. In English he has published comics for Heavy Metal and short stories for the books *Dark Gates* (with Alessandro Manzetti; Kipple, 2014), *My Early Crimes* (Raven's Headpress, 2015), and *The Monster, the Bad and the Ugly* (with Alessandro Manzetti; Kipple, 2016). His short stories have also appeared in *The Beauty of Death Vol. 1* (Independent Legions, 2016), *The Beauty of Death Vol. 2 – Death by Water* (Independent Legions, 2017) and Y*ear's Best Hardcore Horror Volume 2* (Comet Press, 2017). His short story *Hell* is in *The Best Horror of the Year* list by Ellen Datlow (2015). He won the Italian Premio Laymon 2017 (Laymon Award) with his novella *Putridarium*. *Dark Mary* is his first novel translated into English.
He is an active member of the Horror Writers Association and lives in Rome, Italy.
Website: **www.paolodiorazio.com**

000
INDEPENDENT
LEGIONS
PUBLISHING

LATEST BOOK RELEASES

MONSTERS OF ANY KIND

DAVID J. SCHOW
RAMSEY CAMPBELL
JONATHAN MABERRY
EDWARD LEE
LUCY TAYLOR
OWL GOINGBACK
MONICA J. O'ROURKE
CODY GOODFELLOW
DAMIEN ANGELICA WALTERS
MICHAEL BAILEY
BRUCE BOSTON
ERINN L. KEMPER
MARK ALAN MILLER
JESS LANDRY
GREGORY L. NORRIS
GREG SISCO
SANTIAGO EXIMENO
MICHAEL G. BAUGHAN

000
INDEPENDENT
LEGIONS

EDITED BY
ALESSANDRO MANZETTI
AND DANIELE BONFANTI

AVAILABLE BOOKS

Our publications are available at Amazon and major online booksellers. Visit our Website: **www.independentlegions.com**

BOTH PAPERBACK & DIGITAL PUBLICATIONS

TRIBAL SCREAMS
by Owl Goingback

MONSTERS OF ANY KIND
Edited by Alessandro Manzetti & Daniele Bonfanti

KNOWING WHEN TO DIE
by Mort Castle

ARTIFACTS
by Bruce Boston

NARAKA THE ULTIMATE HUMAN BREEDING
by Alessandro Manzetti

A WINTER SLEEP
by Greg F. Gifune

SPREE AND OTHER STORIES
by Lucy Taylor

THE BEAUTY OF DEATH 2 – DEATH BY WATER
edited by Alessandro Manzetti & Jodi Renee Lester

THE LIVING AND THE DEAD
by Greg F. Gifune

THE CARP-FACED BOY AND OTHER TALES
by Thersa Matsuura

THE WISH MECHANICS
by Daniel Braum

CHILDREN OF NO ONE
by Nicole Cushing

THE ONE THAT COMES BEFORE
by Livia Llewellyn

ALL AMERICAN HORROR OF THE 21ST CENTURY: THE FIRST DECADE
Edited by Mort Castle

BENEATH THE NIGHT
by Greg Gifune

SELECTED STORIES
by Nate Southard

FORTHCOMING BOOKS

BOTH PAPERBACK & DIGITAL PUBLICATIONS

FEARFUL SYMMETRIES
by Tom Monteleone

APARTMENT SEVEN
by Greg F. Gifune

CROTA
by Owl Goingback

HORROR CALCUTTA
by Poppy Z. Brite (graphic novel)

COYOTE RAGE
by Owl Goingback

DARK CARNIVAL
by Joanna Parypinski

THE MAN WHO ESCAPED THIS STORY
by Cody Goodfellow

LONG AFTER DARK
by Greg F. Gifune

LOST TRIBE
by Gene O'Neill

DARKER THAN NIGHT
by Owl Goingback

NOT FADE AWAY
by Gene O'Neill

BREED
by Owl Goingback

000 INDEPENDENT LEGIONS
PUBLISHING

INDEPENDENT LEGIONS PUBLISHING
DI ALESSANDRO MANZETTI
Via Virgilio, 10 – TRIESTE (ITALY)
+39 040 9776602

WWW.INDEPENDENTLEGIONS.COM
WWW.FACEBOOK.COM/INDEPENDENTLEGIONS
INDEPENDENT.LEGIONS@AOL.COM

Horror Writers
ASSOCIATION
SPECIALTY PRESS AWARD RECIPIENT